Bridges Revisited

By

K. F. Coffman

This book is a work of fiction. Places, events, and situations in this story are purely fictional. Any resemblance to actual persons, living or dead, is coincidental.

ISBN: 1-4107-5226-7(softcover)
ISBN: 1-4107-5225-9(electronic)
ISBN: 1-4107-5227-5(hardcover)

Library of Congress Control Number: 2003092854

This book is printed on acid free paper.

Printed in the United States of America
Bloomington, IN

1st Books - rev. 05/08/03

Dedication

<u>To Vicki</u>

You are my inspiration, my love,
my life. Without your continued
support and understanding
I would never have to courage
or insight to even try.
With you by my side, all
things are possible. With your
love and devotion, I have found
that I can reach heights most
only dream of reaching. Thank
you for being there for me.
I Love You.
This is for you babe, All for you.

Vicki is pictured on the cover.

Chapter 1

He sat in the middle of the living room floor surrounded by a variety of old magazines and catalogs that had accumulated over the years. Deciding what had expired and what should just go, was sometimes a trick in it's own. The discards all faced the same fate, the dreaded recycling bin out behind the house. As he sorted through all the various publications one stood out, like someone in a crowd yelling your name, something makes you stop and take notice. There, in his hand, was an old National Geographic magazine with a picture of a covered bridge on the cover. The title too stuck out and caught his attention. The Covered Bridges of Madison County Iowa. He, his wife and family had lived in Iowa all their life and not once ever noticed the natural beauty and alluring effect these bridges have on one's soul. The bridge on the cover of the magazine alone seemed to call his name and grip him like a vise. He just couldn't take his eyes off the photo or think about anything but that bridge. We will have to go see these bridges someday he thought as the magazine was tossed in the save pile and the sorting continued. Once done, the discards were tossed in the bin out back and he went about the rest of his day.

Days all seemed to run together as nothing seemed to change except the day and date. He had taken on the role of homemaker about 2 years ago because of a fall resulting in a permanent back injury that would leave him unable to ever work again. His wife of 25 years was now thrown into the role of breadwinner and head of the household whether she wanted it or was ready for it. His days were all the same, get up at 5:30 A.M. to get his wife up for work and start dishes and cleaning the kitchen from whatever was left over from the night before. Let the dog out, start a pot of coffee, turn on the TV and go about getting things done before having to get his oldest son up at 8:00 A.M. for work. After his son left around 8:20 every morning he was on his own for the rest of the day. The only company was the dog, cat, TV and his computer. Every day the same thing, do the dishes, straighten up the house, take out something for dinner and join friends online on his computer. Trying to make life as easy and effortless for his wife as he could, he knew that all of this was starting to take its toll on even her. Day's turned into weeks, weeks into months and so on, never seeming to end.

1

The last 2 years had taken a toll not only on the family finances and everyday living but on their relationship also. It seemed that he and his wife just went through the motions of living together and the arrangement was becoming more one of convenience than anything. At times it was like living with your sister or a room mate. Like living with an old familiar friend that you have known your entire life, and for the time being, it seemed as though this was as good as it would get. Their children, all grown, and all but one living away and on their own, it was just the two of them most of the time.

Ken, 46, had been working in management at the time of his accident and had tried to go back to work with no avail. Everything he and the doctors tried failed and soon his wife Nikki, 42, had to assume the role of breadwinner. It was a difficult task to take on at this point in her life and it killed him inside to see his beautiful wife have to support him. She should be at home enjoying herself with the grandchildren, and, kids stopping by from time to time. Instead, she was worrying if she would get any overtime this week so they could pay the bills. On top of that, if they went anywhere, she had to worry about getting his wheelchair out of the car and pushing him through the stores and such. This too was more than he could bear at times, she shouldn't have to do this with a man this young. We should be planning weekend getaways and mini vacations and enjoying our time alone. Instead we worry about handicapped parking, wheelchair accessability and whether he would be able to be on his feet long enough to even enjoy the trip in the first place. Put this all together and you definitely have the recipe for "as good as it gets".

After his daily work was done and his friends on the computer knew that he was, in fact, still alive, Ken sits down to watch some TV and count the hours until his wife returns from work. Longing for company that doesn't growl and bark or meow, he picks up the magazine and again looks at the covered bridge on the cover. He decides to check out the article and see if it tells just where these amazing bridges are located. Maybe they are close enough to make a weekend getaway of it after all. He knows that his wife would enjoy just getting away from kids, work, phones and everyday routine for a day or two and thought that if these bridges were, in fact, close enough to make a day of it, that might make for a pleasant surprise. Reading the article, he finds that there are 6 of these covered bridges left in a county within 2 hours of where they live. That could be a very nice weekend away together if he could arrange it without her knowing about it. As a matter of fact, they had passed right through this county before on several occasions and never realized that these bridges existed. This would be his goal, to put together a weekend of bridges, room- service, and being alone and away from all the everyday problems that shadow their lives on a daily basis. But where would he start? How would he arrange it without her knowing? How could he be sure she wouldn't make plans herself for weekend activities that would result in disaster for his "bridges" getaway?

To accomplish this he would have to be resourceful, sneaky, cunning, and at times maybe even a little diabolical. This would be a weekend for just them. At worst, it would be a nice change of pace, that would get them away for a couple of days, something they had never done before. If it wasn't raising kids or helping with grandchildren, something else always seemed to stop them from doing anything remotely like this. Then his accident and not being able to work or do any activities for long periods of time, it just seemed that anything like this would be out of the question. At best, maybe this would bring back some magic their relationship seemed to have lost over the last couple of years and give them a fresh start. Either way it couldn't hurt to just pick up and get away from everything for a weekend and be alone together, really alone.

The computer was the first place he headed to check out the bridges and county information. This is, after all, the age of technology and information, and everything seemed to be on the Internet anymore. It might be a long shot, but at least it is a place to start. The magazine was after all, an old 1965 issue. He wasn't even sure of how they got it or where it came from. Here goes nothing he thought as he signed on line and did a search for Iowa counties. There it was, a link for Madison County, could it really be this easy? I guess we will find out. Clicking on the link, he found information on all 6 bridges, motels and restaurant information and activities that go on throughout the entire year. This might be easier than he thought, now to start scheming. First we have to find a weekend that could work for us to slip away unnoticed, as it were. Looking at the calender and deciding on the weekend of his birthday, he picked up the phone and called his daughter. She would be the only one that could put a kink in his plans, if she and the grandchildren had any plans that involved the two of them, this could definitely be a problem. His daughter, Lynn, answered the phone and he began to lay out his plan to get her mother, Nikki, away for the weekend. She cleared the way to proceed with his plans as she explained that she and her husband were taking the kids up to her in laws for the weekend and wouldn't be home anyway. This was starting to look like it might work after all.

With the weekend cleared of any surprise plans for the moment, he turned to his son next. "What do you have planned for this next weekend" he asked? Kenny Jr told his dad that he had plans to visit a friend for the weekend and he wouldn't be home himself until late Sunday night. This is too good to be true he thought. Finally his plan might take shape and work after all. Jr told his dad that he in fact was wondering if they could go out to dinner Thursday night for his birthday so he could leave Friday evening right after work. "I know Friday is actually your birthday, but, if it's ok with you, could we go to dinner Thursday instead"? "Just you and Mom and I". Ken almost jumped for joy, this is working out much too easy he thought. Something has to come up at the last moment and spoil everything. The youngest child, his son Will was away at boot camp in the Air Force and he knew that nothing would spring up unexpectedly on that end. Now for the final step, find out if she has to work Friday without making her suspicious and asking a lot of questions.

When Nikki arrived home from work, he asked if she had to work Friday or if this was going to be another 4-day week? She informed him that they were only working 4 days this week and she had Friday off. Asking why, he hurriedly told her that he was just wondering if they might have plans for his birthday Friday or if she had to work. She told him that she planned on them going out to dinner and maybe a drive or something and asked if that would be ok with him. He assured her that it would be fine and told her of Jr's plans for dinner Thursday and Lynn's plans to go to her in laws for the weekend. "Looks like it might just be us for the weekend then" she told him. He smiled an impish smile and told her that just being alone for the weekend to relax and do nothing would be fine with him. If she knew what he was really up to she would probably have a fit. He knew that they couldn't really afford to do this, but, for some unknown reason, he also knew he had to. It was as though something were drawing him to these spectacular bridges. He just hoped that he would find out what this magical, mystical draw to the bridges would be all about this weekend. Why was he so drawn to them, was there something that no one could foresee or imagine involved? Only time would tell and he was determined to get the answers for himself.

After everyone left for work the next day Ken got down to business and started making calls. First he would have to find a motel and make reservations for Friday and Saturday, then he would want to get information as fast as possible on the bridges and their actual locations within the county. The first call was to the local Chamber of Commerce, they should have the information he was seeking. To his surprise, they had maps and brochures on the bridges and all the local attractions available. They told him they could even fax them to him if he had a fax readily available to him. He told them he did and gave them his fax number. Soon he was receiving faxes with motel and dining information, locations and maps of the bridges, and, some events that go on during the year. Complete with phone numbers and reservation information he rapidly sprang into action. First calling motels. Unfortunately, the first one he called was booked that weekend due to a family reunion in town, and, they weren't sure if the other motel in town would be booked or not. This didn't look good he thought. Deciding not to give up so easily, he called the second motel and found they in fact had 1 room left for that weekend. Needless to say, he reserved it immediately.

Now armed with maps and directions to these amazing bridges and some interesting facts about them, the motel reserved for the weekend and no family plans to interfere with his quest, he sat back and started planning a romantic weekend alone with his beautiful wife. What would they do first? Where would they go, and, what would they see? Would this be the weekend to rekindle their romance or a flop that should be chocked up to a bad idea? So many questions and no answers yet. I guess only time will tell he thought, only time will tell. One thing was for certain he thought, he was being beckoned to this area and these bridges for a reason. One that he couldn't explain nor understand at this time, but, his mind was made up to get these and a lot of other answers this weekend. One thing was very clear to him though, he knew for some untold, unknown reason they had to make this trip. Of that he was very certain and knew that he couldn't, no, wouldn't let a chance go by to get something back that seemed to be lost. He owed that and more to her. He owed it to them both.

Chapter 2

Ken, a big man at 6'2" and about 300 pounds with a balding spot in the back, grey hair, beard and mustache always kept neatly groomed and trimmed, was repeatedly mistaken for Santa Clause by his oldest grand daughter. He is a big man that is somewhat frightening at first glance. Hardened face and steel blue eyes that had the ability to look straight through you if he so chose. Yet he had a heart as big as he was, and, was the gentlest, kindest, most easy going man that you could ever want to meet. At first appearance he looks as though he would rip off your head for even speaking to him and after getting to know him, you find that he would in fact give you his last scrap of food and the shirt off his very back if he thought it would help you out. He has a love of life and a devotion to his friends and family that is actually very rare in people today. He likes to sit with his grandchildren and watch the birds, flowers, clouds and the natural beauty of everything he sees in life itself. No one would ever believe something like this of this giant of a man, but, he finds the good in everyone and the beauty in even the most awful circumstance. He has an infectious laugh that makes everyone laugh with him and hates to see anyone hurt or sad and does everything in his power to make you feel good about yourself and leave with a smile. He is the complete opposite of everything you would first think about him and likes it that way. With the business ethics of a man from years in the past, he still believes that a man's word and a hand shake are better than any written contract. You don't quite know how to take him or what to think when you first meet, but, even a short time with him, leaves you feeling as though you can't wait for him to return.

Nikki, his wife for what seems like forever, for both of them, is somewhat tall for a woman. 5'8" tall and a very slender 135 pounds, with long blonde hair that cascades down to the middle of her back in waves and the deepest blue eyes you could imagine. She is a 42-year old mother and grandmother, and looks more like her 24 year old daughters sister than her Mom. A very beautiful, sexy, vibrant woman that is as full of mischief as a 4-year old and as adventuresome as a 10 year old boy. Full of fire and energy, she could wear out even the most fit and vigorous teenagers. She likes spontaneity, doing things on the spur of the moment, even if it means taking a certain amount of risk with it. She is adventurous, never backing down from a challenge or adventure, and has a temper that would make Lucifer himself run for cover. She is protective of what is hers and no one ever, and I mean ever, messes with her family. That is the one thing that is certain, she would fight to the death for her family. She is impatient, she wants everything and she wants it right now. And couldn't be a better match for Ken.

Thrown together when they both were much too young to even think about marriage, let alone, beginning a family together. Nikki was only 17 at the time and Ken was almost 21. Everyone that knew them took bets that they would either be divorced or kill each other within a year. 25 years, 3 children and 3 grandchildren later, they are still going strong with no end in sight. The road they took to get to this point was indeed a very rocky and treacherous path to say the least. More than one time they almost packed it in and walked the other way, never to look back again. Somehow, something kept them together through all of this, and more, and made them the couple they are today. Once again though, uncertainty and fear was driving a wedge between them that is obvious yet unseen. Without speaking a single word they both knew that the threat was real and definitely present. How would they get through this? Would this be the end finally? So many questions and no answers anywhere made this even more unbearable at times. She wouldn't say a word yet you could unmistakably see it written on her beautiful face. He never said a word either, yet, you knew he was at his wits end and just couldn't quite grasp the solution to this problem. How could he get them back? How could he show her that she was still the most important part of his life? She was in fact, his entire life. Somehow, someway, he knew that he would be able to do this. Lately the words to assure and comfort her just weren't there anymore. He hoped the bridges and their weekend trip would show them both that the most important ingredients in their very lives, were in fact each other.

The only thing standing in their way now would be an unexpected change at work and Nikki being called in on Friday after all. Keeping his fingers crossed and praying for the best, he started counting down the days until he could put his plan into action. Silently and secretly he started packing clothes that he knew she wouldn't miss, or wear, until her days off. As for himself, he could pretty much get everything ready Thursday before they left without her noticing anything of his missing from the laundry. This is going to work he thought, it has to work. With that in mind he packed clothes for her, enough for 3 days. Her makeup and their personal toiletries would prove to be the trickiest items as she would want to use hers the morning they leave, so, packing them was pretty much out of the question. With that in mind, he set about doing everything he could without drawing any attention from her or anyone else for that matter. He didn't need anyone starting to ask a lot of questions that he would have to answer in front of her. That could prove to be disastrous.

As he went about his everyday tasks and chores, dishes, cleaning the house and planning meals, one question kept haunting him. Where did that old National Geographic come from? Could it be something they picked up in a doctors office somewhere and just threw it in with the rest of the magazines and catalogs? And why, in heavens name, did he have a 1965 issue of this magazine? This just made no sense to him. That would have been something he would have thrown out years ago, and yet, there it was in the basket with the rest. To make things even more confusing, why was it an issue of the covered bridges of Madison County Iowa? He had lived in Iowa all of his life and faintly remembers others talking briefly about these bridges, yet he had no interest in seeing them, until now. Suddenly it was all he could think about, as though something or someone was unmistakably drawing him toward these magnificent bridges. He just hoped to find the answers to these and other questions when he got there. It would be an interesting journey, of that he was sure. As for the answers to his questions, that would have to be seen.

The days passing quickly and uneventful, no one had a clue yet to his master plan, of this he was sure. If she had any idea that something was being planned she would speak up and have a million questions. Patience, he thought, was never a virtue his wife was accused of possessing. She has always been the type that has to know everything and has to know now. Even Christmas at their house was never a surprise, she always had to know what she was getting and from whom. You just couldn't surprise her or pull something like this off without her knowing about it. He was very proud of himself for being able to keep the secret from her this long without drawing attention or suspicions. He never could keep anything from her before, they talked to each other about everything, even if it could mean an argument would follow, they still told each other everything.

Here it is Thursday already, they leave tomorrow and she knows nothing. He almost jumped at the thought of this fantastic feat he had done. Keeping a secret from Nikki, that was almost a super human feat in its own right. Her bag was packed and put away, his was ready also. The real test would come in the morning when he got her makeup and things together and packed without her knowing anything. If he pulled that off, he would be home free. Tomorrow would be the final test. Getting her in the car and on the road without her suspecting anything out of the ordinary until they were well on their way. He felt confident that he could pull it off, he had so far. Nikki came home from work that evening and dinner was ready. Dishes were done, house clean, and everything was in order and lay in waiting for his surprise trip in the morning. Now, to get her out of the house and on the road, what could he tell her? How could he do this without drawing suspicion from her? It would almost take a miracle to pull that one off, and at that point, the phone rang, it was their daughter Lynn.

Lynn, her husband and 3 children live about half an hour north of her parents. Nikki didn't like the idea of them moving out of town as she doesn't see the grandchildren as often as she would like. They used to live just 2 blocks away and she saw them almost daily, now, she sees them on weekends unless they go out of town to see his parents, which they were doing this weekend. The miracle Ken needed just arrived. Lynn was asking her mom to bring some things up that she left at the house the last time they were down. "I need the kids' life jackets and swimsuits that we left the last time we were there, could you bring them up to me in the morning so we can leave as soon as he gets off work"? Nikki doesn't appear to be utterly joyed at the idea of having to do this, but then again, it gives her a chance to see the kids for a while too. Reluctantly she says she will bring the things up and will do it in the morning because she has things she wants to do around home. There is the miracle he needed, Ken looks toward the ceiling and silently whispers "Thank You". Now the last piece of the puzzle just fell into place, nothing could go wrong now, nothing could stop his plan from working he thought. At that particular moment he was so very proud of himself. 25 years with this woman and I'm finally going to do something special for her, a surprise that he was sure she would love and she didn't have the slightest idea that anything was going on.

10

The next morning Nikki slept in as Ken showered, made sure the dishes and house were all in order, the animals fed and watered and everything that could be packed was already in the car. The only thing left to do was pack makeup and personal things they would need and they would be off. He had filled the car with gas the night before, filled the cooler with soda's and ice and stashed it in the car late last night as she slept. Down the hall he heard her stirring and asked if she wanted some coffee to help her wake up, she gladly accepted. With her in the shower, Ken walked through the house to make sure he hadn't forgotten anything. Everything was ready, except his wife. Nikki quickly showered, dressed and put on her makeup, brushed her teeth and was ready to face the day. As she sat and drank her coffee and woke up a bit, Ken slipped into the bathroom, put her makeup and their things in a bag, and slipped it between the wall and linen cabinet so she wouldn't stumble upon it. This is it he thought, I am going to pull this off yet. While Nikki was in the bedroom making the bed, he slipped the final bag into the car and was ready to spring his plan into action. The day was finally here. Nikki asked if he was going with her to see the kids and they would catch lunch and come home. He gladly said yes and they locked the house, jumped in the car and headed for their daughter's house. As they pulled away, he noticed that he had put the National Geographic issue about the bridges in the car with them and couldn't remember, nor explain, why he had done it. As they drove Nikki picked up the old issue and started thumbing through it. Look, she exclaimed, these old bridges are right here in Iowa. We will have to go see them someday. Little did she know that her someday would be today.

The drive to their daughters was about usual, same scenery, same roads, nothing out of the ordinary. Nikki had wished him a Happy Birthday as soon as the car cleared the driveway and other than normal small talk between them on the ride up, the only other thing posed to him was where they would eat lunch. This is, after all, your day she told him and I want you to pick out where we go today. If only she really knew what was in store for her that day, the trip, the bridges, the thought of being really alone for 3 whole days. This was going to be the best birthday he had ever had he thought as he drove along. If only he knew what they would find on their journey over the next few days and what lye ahead for them, this was truly about to be his best birthday yet, he just didn't know it yet.

K. F. Coffman

Chapter 3

As they pulled in the drive of their daughter's house, they were instantly met by 3 children waving and jumping almost hysterically. They looked at each other, smiled, started to laugh, and simultaneously said "they're yours". As the car came to a stop and the doors opened, they both were mobbed by 3 screaming children. Grandpa, Grandma they yelled. Hugs and kisses and birthday wishes from all out of the way, they took the kids into the house to see their daughter. "Happy Birthday Dad" she yelled as soon as Ken came through the door. With a big hug, a birthday kiss and a piece of lemon meringue pie in hand, she led her father to the kitchen table and lit a single candle on the pie. Make a wish and blow out your candle he was told. Closing his eyes and making his wish, he once again opened his eyes to find 3 giddy children helping grandpa blow that single candle out. Clapping for joy as the fire extinguished, he was now handed birthday cards and presents and another round of hugs and kisses from his grandchildren. Today was indeed starting off to be one of the best he could remember in a very long time and it was only the beginning he thought. Maybe wishes really do come true, if so, his would be to give his beautiful bride a weekend that she would remember for the rest of her life, and his for that matter.

A few hours passed and it was finally time to be on the road again. This time Nikki thought would be their lunch stop, then home. Thinking of what she could do for her husband that night that would be special and surprising. She could only come up with dinner, maybe a drive, and, an evening watching movies with buttered popcorn and a new nightie. After lunch, she would ask Ken if they could go shopping for a while? I need to pick up a few things if you don't mind. It was fine with him, he actually enjoyed shopping with his wife. They always acted like little kids in a candy store with a dollar for the first time whenever they went shopping. They had to hit every store, look at each and every thing in it, find all of the off the wall and oddball things they could find and try to figure out who could we give this to or where could we put this? It was almost comical watching them shop, you never could figure out who was worse, him or her. Most of the time it would come out a draw.

Noticing that it was still a bit early for lunch, as it was only around 11:00 in the morning, he announced to Nikki that he would like to drive out to a small town they frequented that had tons of antiques and collectibles in the shops and then they would catch lunch. Eagerly she agreed, she loved to browse the old shops and look at all the antiques and oddities they always seemed to find on these outings. As he drove along, he noticed that Nikki was staring out the window and seemed to be about to nod off for a bit. This would be perfect he thought, if she takes a short nap, he could be at their final destination before she wakes and realizes that she doesn't know where they are. With this in mind, Ken turns on an easy listening rock station they like and lets her nod off. Not only would this give him the time he needed to get where he was going, but, he also knew that she really needed the sleep. She works hard both at work and home and the weekends aren't always the rest and relaxation she would like, so he let her sleep. Not only that he thought, but, she will be more alert and ready to make an evening of it if she gets even a short nap.

He drove along listening to the music trying his best not to wake his sleeping bride. She looks so beautiful he thought, how did I ever get so lucky? He sees the sign telling him his exit is only 2 more miles. He slows and exits and comes to the stop sign at the bottom of the exit ramp. The sign says the town he is looking for is 16 miles to the right. He turns and gets up to speed quickly as not to awake her from lack of motion in the car. She stirs a bit but drops back off quickly and is deep in sleep again. The countryside is lush and green with trees and plants and the rolling hills seem to be never ending. This is so beautiful he thinks to himself. I have lived here all my life and never noticed the beauty that lies only a couple of hours from home. Seems like that's always the way it is though, you never notice what is right beyond your yard because you take it for granted. Up and down the hills he drives, as he tops the last hill, he notices a large dome of what looks like a capital or courthouse ahead. This must be the courthouse they talk about in the literature he received, it said the dome could be seen for miles, and it appears as though they were right.

Entering town he stops at the 4-way stop sign. The intersection of the 2 major highways that ran through the little town. Nikki wakes and stretches and looks around. "Where in the world are we", she asks? "Well, to tell you the truth my love, I'm glad you slept through the trip". "I wasn't quite sure of how I was going to explain all this when we missed our exit back down the road and I knew you would have a million questions". "Your nap sure saved me a lot of explaining". With a sheepish smile, she stretched again, sat up in the seat, turned to her husband, and asked again in a bit more forceful voice, "where are we honey"? Just then he noticed the building on his right that said Chamber of Commerce, Tourist Information Center. He pulled up in front of the building and turned to his wife and said "welcome to Winterset, Iowa my sweet". "Winterset", she exclaimed, "isn't that the place where all those covered bridges are"? He smiled from ear to ear and just said "why yes my dear, it is". Now she knew she had been had. How did he ever pull this off without me knowing about it she thought? I always find out before he can pull something over on me. I must be slipping she thought as they got out of the car and went inside.

Stepping through the door was almost like stepping back in time. The building was an old 1800's building with some updating and modernization done, that was evident. Racks lined the walls with brochures of local and statewide attractions, maps of the bridge locations, and old pictures of what the town looked like years ago and the progress it has seen since. Sitting behind the desk was a short, silver haired lady that greeted you as soon as the door closed and treated you like she had known you all her life. "Hello, welcome to Winterset" she exclaimed, "make sure you sign our guest book." Ken told her they were there to see the bridges and she reached for a map and showed them just where and how to get to every single one. She told them about other points of interest in town and in the county itself and told them no trip would be complete unless you took the time to see it all. Armed with even more literature and maps now, they exited the building and returned to the car. Putting the information away, Ken looked up the street and noticed a diner. "Let's eat lunch there" he told his wife, looking at the diner she agreed wholeheartedly as she was hungry and ready for lunch. They entered the diner and again felt as though they had just entered a time warp. The inside looked as though it was still in the 1960's with some modern equipment set about. By reading the information on the way and looking at the pictures lining the walls, they learned that the diner had opened in the late 1800's and hadn't been through much remodeling since. With a counter to the left lined with antique stools, and booths lining the wall to the right, they chose a booth and sat down. They looked at the menu, ordered lunch and sat back to sip their water and wait.

"How in the world did you pull this off without me catching you" Nikki asked? "It wasn't easy, that's for sure" Ken told her. "You always seem to know everything and I was certain that I would never get this done without you finding out". "How long are we here for? Just the day or what"? "That's the best part honey, we are here for the whole weekend, just the 2 of us". "I already have a room for the weekend and plan on seeing all the bridges and everything else the area has to offer". "Did I do good" Ken asked? "Yes silly, you did great, we both really needed to do something like this and you know it". Whew, he breathed a sigh of relief, this was just what the doctor ordered he thought. Just then lunch was set before them and they enjoyed their meal with the sights and sounds of the locals in the diner swirling about them. After lunch they went to find their motel and get checked in, after all, it would be easier dropping everything but the camera off now and not having to worry so much about keeping the car in sight at all times. This would just seem to make things easier for both of them, so, they set out to find their room. Finding the motel was easier than he thought, he just asked the cashier in the diner and she gave him front door directions.

The motel was fairly new and the room was great. A queen bed, 2 night stands, a desk for writing postcards to the kids and letters to their son in the Air Force and a recliner to watch TV from. "Hey" Ken exclaimed, "it even has a remote for the TV". Nikki just rolled her eyes and told him that if he thought he was going to sit in that recliner and watch TV, she was going back home now. "No, No, my dear" he said, "the thought never crossed my mind". "Yeah right" she said, and, they were on the road again in search of their first bridge. Closing the door behind her, Nikki asked which bridge they should start with? "Let's go to the furthest ones first and work our way back toward town". Sounded like a plan to her, so, they started the car and their search for road signs began.

Chapter 4

The maps and directions they had were actually very accurate and detailed. Not thinking it would be that easy, this turned out to be a plus indeed. They found the first bridge, the Hogback Bridge. The information they had said the bridge is in it's original location and was built in 1884. They read about the bridges as they strolled from one side to the other, as the bridges were now closed off to traffic. It again made them feel as if they had stepped back in time. It was interesting reading about the bridges and discovering that they were covered to preserve the flooring planks. It seems the lumber used in the floors was very hard and expensive to replace, and, they found that covering them was an economical way to save these planks. They found it far cheaper to replace the roof and sides of the bridge than the floor planking. Walking hand in hand through the bridge and marveling at the construction and how cool it was inside, compared to the sweltering heat of a typical July summer day in Iowa outside, they both found it nice to have the bridge all to themselves. This was, after all, an early Friday afternoon and most people were either still working or hadn't invaded the town for the weekend yet. They walked and talked about how it must have been to live in these past times when using these bridges was an everyday occurrence. The lazy river running beneath them, the reflection of this majestic old bridge in the water were captivating to say the least. As they once again reached the car, they looked at the map to plan their strategy to the next target. "Let's go to the Cedar bridge next" Ken said. It says in the brochure they still allow traffic on it. Nikki agreed as it was on the northern edge of town, and, they were already a couple of miles north of town as it were.

The Cedar Bridge was nestled in a small and quaint park on the northern edge of Winterset. The bridge was surrounded by trees and shrubbery and took you back to slower and easier times. They drove over the bridge, got out, walked back across to take in the scenery and the Cedar Creek below. Again, they had the bridge all to themselves and took in the lines and construction of this old bridge and imagined themselves in another time. It was true what they say about these old bridges, they say they bring people together, and it was plain to see that they had this very affect on this couple. Taking his wife in his arms and stealing a kiss inside the bridge, Ken looked deep into Nikki's eyes and said "I Love You babe", she was so glad he tricked her into this weekend trip, he would have no idea how glad she was until later she thought. "I Love You to Ken" she told him and kissed him again as they walked back to the car wrapped in each others arms. I have an idea, he said, I'll walk back across and take pictures as you drive the car across. The kids will love seeing Mom drive across an old, covered bridge like this. "Don't forget your cane" she told him as he hadn't used it at the last stop and was supposed to use it if he wasn't in his wheelchair. She worried about him constantly and nagged him to no end about this. Hesitantly, he got his cane out of the car, smiled and said "yes dear, I'll be good" and strolled back across to ready himself for the picture. She hesitantly agreed and got the car. The camera clicked away as he snapped several pictures of her driving across the bridge. "That takes care of that roll" he told her as she picked him up on the other side. "We have already used a roll of film" she asked. "Yep, between the pictures we took at the Hogback and the Cedar, we finished our first roll sweetheart". "We need more film" she said as they headed back to town to shop.

Finding a place to shop wasn't a problem for Nikki, she could find a place to shop in the middle of the Sahara dessert Ken thought. They found a department store in town and decided to see what they had to offer. If I know my wife, he thought, I can rest assured that she will find more than just film to buy. With that he smiled and followed her into the store like a careless child following a playful puppy. Inside they found a motorized cart for their handicapped shoppers and Ken got on. They investigated the camera department and agreed to buy several rolls of film as they were determined to see each and every bridge and that meant lots of pictures. After all, who would believe that he pulled all this off without her having a clue unless he had the photo evidence to prove it. They wandered each aisle and found some other necessities they just had to have, you know, like the writing tablet that she needed to write a letter to Will in boot camp and things like that. Of course she had two dozen tablets at home, but then again, they weren't at home, were they? After snacks, film, some clearance items that just couldn't be passed up and things he didn't even know were in the basket, they proceeded to the checkout counter. "You must be in town to see the bridges" the girl at the counter asked, "why yes, how could you ever have guessed" Ken asked? Not many of the locals come in and buy 10 rolls of film she replied. "Dead giveaway huh" he asked? Pretty much was her reply as she continued to ring their purchases up and total the bill. They all laughed as he handed her his credit card and signed the receipt. Make sure you see all of them the lady added, they really are something to see. They nodded and waved and headed for the car with basket in tow. Now back to the motel to unload again he told Nikki, she agreed and they headed for the room.

Once all the bags from the car were placed securely in the room, Nikki flopped back on the bed and stared at the ceiling. "What's wrong babe" Ken asked? "Nothing" she replied, "still can't believe you pulled this all off without me suspecting something, but, I'm sure glad you did". "Thank you again for such a wonderful surprise" she told her husband. "What's next" he asked? "Another bridge, or do we try to find a place to eat and relax and take in the square in town"? Dinner was starting to really sound like a safe bet at this point and the town square really was pretty and had lots of interesting looking old shops lining the streets. "Dinner and more shopping sounds like a plan to me" Nikki said. He knew better than to even ask he thought, "when will I ever learn" he asked himself? "Ok then, dinner and shopping it is". "The diner sound good or do you want to explore the town and see what else they may have"? The diner was comfortable and somehow familiar already and in some strange way already felt like their place in this strange town. "The diner", she squealed as she jumped from the bed and headed toward the door. "I guess we are eating at the diner" he thought as he closed and locked the door and followed her to the car.

They entered the diner and quickly found a booth not far from the one they sat and ate lunch in. Sliding in and picking up menus, Nikki said "look, we have the same waitress we had for lunch". It was true the same kind, older, grey-haired lady sauntered over to the table with water glasses in hand and smiled and asked "you two back already"? They both grinned and giggled and said they just couldn't stay away. "I'll give you some time to look and be back in a bit" she told them. They discussed the menu, decided on dinner, and calmly waited for her return. "What will it be tonight folks" the slender lady asked the couple. They placed their order and engaged in small talk awaiting their choices to arrive at the table. They quietly ate dinner and mapped out a strategy for the remaining bridges and what order they would see them in. The waitress saw the maps of the county and literature about the bridges scattered about the tabletop and asked if the couple had come to see the bridges. "Yes" they chimed in, "we have lived in Iowa all our lives and never made it over to see them". The older lady asked if she could join them, and, told them she could show them the easiest and fastest way to reach each one and could tell them a little about them, if they didn't mind. "No" they happily exclaimed, they would be more than happy to hear some inside scoop on the old bridges and the shortcuts would be nice to know about too.

As they sat and talked about each one and the history behind them, Ken could tell that something was going untold about a couple of the bridges. "Excuse me, but if you don't mind me asking, you seem to either be saving the best for last or purposely skipping over a couple of these old bridges". "Is there something we should know about them or something you don't want us to know"? "No, not really" she told them. "If you are really interested in hearing the story as I know it, I would be more than happy to tell you what I either know, have heard, or know to be fact about two of the bridges". They almost jumped at once and told her they were all ears. They looked at each other and couldn't help but wonder what deep dark secret the two bridges held. Was it a dark, town secret not told to outsiders but a lucky few or something they couldn't begin to grasp? They couldn't wait for the woman to tell her story. "Well", she started out, "the story is, back in the middle 60's a local farmers wife and a photographer that was just passing through on an assignment met, fell in love, and had a torrid affair for four days". "I know how sordid and dirty that sounds" she continued, "but, it really wasn't like that at all". "The story went untold until the woman's death and her children came back to the area here and found her diaries". "Now, I have to tell you that most of the people involved have either moved away or passed on, so, verifying any of the story would be almost impossible at best". They sat back and listened to the tale the best this kind, old woman could remember it. The story as told goes something like this.

Late summer in Madison county Iowa was hot, hazy and non-eventful for the most part. The woman's name was Francesca, and, she was the wife of a local farmer, Richard. Richard had taken the couple's two children, a boy and a girl, to the Illinois state fair to show livestock and Francesca stayed behind to have four whole days to herself to clean and just relax. Something that was a rarity usually, as time to herself just wasn't something that she was accustomed to, so, she jumped at the chance when it arose. The day after her family left brought a photographer to her door, lost and looking for directions. His name was Robert something, she really couldn't recall his last name as it had been so many years ago. He was an older, tall, slender, greying man that was on assignment from some magazine to take pictures of the bridges here in Madison county. He was kind of a loner, wanderer type, that none of us around the town or county saw much. We knew he was here, we knew why he was here, but, it just seemed that you never really saw much of him. Anyway, back to the story she said. He stopped at the little farm to ask directions to one of the bridges and Francesca did her best to help. Something was lost in the translation though, she was originally from Italy and still had problems with some of her English at times. This made it rather hard to understand her at times and this just happened to be one of them. It is told that she offered to show him the way to the bridge as the roads weren't marked and like all other locals, it's easier to show you than tell you. He eagerly accepted her offer and off they went to the Roseman bridge.

Upon arriving at the bridge, he decided that the lighting wasn't right to start taking pictures then and was to come back the next morning at dawn. He drove Francesca home and thanked her for her help. He was about to leave and rumor has it that she asked him to stay for diner. Being a stranger in these parts and on the road quite a bit, he gladly accepted and joined her. From what has been told, after an evening of laughter and drinks Robert left as he had to be up very early to get the shots he needed for the magazine. It appears that Francesca drove to the Roseman bridge that same night. She left him a note asking him back for dinner again that very next night. During his photo session at the bridge he finds the note and calls to let her know that he would love to join her again, but, would be late as he was going to the Holliwell bridge next and wanted to get things laid out before he lost all daylight. I guess she agreed to meet him at the bridge and they would return together to her house and have dinner. It appears that she drove to Des Moines, bought a new dress and returned to her farm to get yet another call from her new friend. He told her that if the gossip of meeting him would be too much for her, he would understand her not wanting to meet him at the bridge. She assured him that it would not be a problem and she still planned on meeting him. From there the details get pretty fuzzy, but, it was told that this would be the first night they would make love together. It would be the first night she had ever cheated on her husband and Robert himself was entering a world he had no experience in. He had never done anything like this before, but, it has been told that he was starting to have feelings for her that he could neither deny nor explain.

The rest of the story is, they spent the next 3 days together and fell deeply and passionately in love. They spent the days exploring the countryside together and found spots to have some much needed privacy. The nights they spent at her farm living and loving like there would be no tomorrow, because for them, the tomorrow's were indeed limited. They both knew that her family would return, Robert would leave, and nothing would ever be the same again for either of them. Richard returned home with the children, Robert left town without her and was to never be heard from again, or so we thought. Seems that after his death, he was cremated and had his ashes thrown off the Roseman bridge. We all found out later that Francesca also was cremated and had her ashes thrown from the Roseman to be with Robert for the rest of eternity. The story is about two people that meet, fall deeply and completely in love in just four short days, and are to never again be together until their ashes are thrown off the bridge for all eternity. Small town gossip and rumors run rampant as I'm sure you both know, but this was different some how. Nothing was ever said to dirty or sully the reputations of either person and it's almost as though the whole county understood and accepted it. "The only thing I can add to this" the waitress said as she rose and started to walk away, is, "his story appeared in an issue of the National Geographic magazine and Francesca's children donated a book that Robert had published with pictures about those four wonderful days in it". "It is in the library and you could check it out tomorrow if you'd like to". With that she picked up their plates, laid down their dinner check and told the couple goodnight, and disappeared to the back of the diner. Nikki and Ken looked at each other with mouths dropped open, it was Ken that spoke first. "Are you thinking what I am thinking" he asked? Nikki could only nod her head yes, that old National Geographic magazine in the car, it had to be the one, but, how did we get it and how did it bring us here? Still a lot of questions and as of yet, not enough answers.

Chapter 5

They drove back to the room, almost in complete silence, Ken reached into the back seat, took out the magazine and went straight to their room. Once inside the couple laid across the bed together and opened the front cover. There inside was an article about Robert and his pictorial on the bridges of Madison county. They read the article and looked at the picture of Robert before them, it was Ken that said something first. "Look, honey, he is wearing some sort of necklace, a cross with writing on it". "I can't make out what it says though". Reaching into one of their bags he retrieves a magnifying glass and returns next to his wife on the bed. "Here, see if you can make out what it says" he tells her as he hands his wife the object. "Oh My God, you will not believe this" she shrieks, "you won't believe this in a million-years Ken". "What, what is it babe?" Nikki turns to him, eyes wide open, mouth dropped open and stutters something. "What did you say" he asks again? She composes herself a bit and tells him that the writing on the necklace is a name. "It just says Francesca" she tells him. They look at each other in disbelief and amazement. "So, this story appears to have more truth to it than I thought" he tells her. "I really wasn't sure about it at first, I mean, it could have been some tall tale spun for the tourists about these long lost lovers and their two bridges to make them want to stay a little longer and visit more of the sights". "It must be true then" Nikki says, "it has to be". "We will do our best to find out starting tomorrow morning" Ken tells her, "we will do our best sweetheart".

Nikki slips into the bathroom and changes into a sheer little neglige she bought at the store when they stopped. "So that's one of those clearance items you just had to have huh" Ken asks. Posing and twirling a bit as if a French model on a runway in Paris, she asks "do you like it"? "What do you think" is his only response as he reaches out and takes her hand and gently pulls her next to him on the bed. They kiss passionately and deeply and find some sort of new fire deep within their very being and meld together as one. After making love totally and completely, they lay in each others arms and fall fast asleep. Ken can only smile and think to himself that this was indeed a very good idea to come here.

Ken was the first to wake that next morning. He sat in the recliner and watched his beautiful wife sleep in the bed next to him. Remembering the night before and how much passion they both felt. She looks like an Angel he thinks to himself and smiles. He has never lost touch with just how lucky he is to have this woman in his life. Of that he has always been sure, even through some of the roughest and most trying times. He thanks God and counts his blessings each and every day, even though she might not be aware of that. He decides to go down to the front desk and get some fresh coffee and let her sleep. She doesn't get much of a chance to do that with work and taking care of the house and him, so, when the opportunity arises to let her sleep in, he always lets her enjoy it. Today would be no different he thought as he poured a cup of coffee and headed back to the room. He slipped in quietly and sat down to read the article on the bridges again. How in the world did he ever get this magazine and what brought them to this area? He couldn't explain it, nor could he understand it, but one thing was for sure, they had been much closer all day yesterday than they had in a long time. It seems as though just being here has already, some how, made them closer and for that he was glad and wasn't about to question it. His mind wandering to a million places at once and thoughts running through his head so fast he couldn't sort them out, something brought him back to reality. Nikki was stirring in the bed next to him, as he looked over at his wife, she was watching him and smiling.

"Morning, sleepy-head" he told her, "did you sleep well last night"? She told him she did but visions of Robert and Francesca kept weaving in and out of her dreams all night long. "I just couldn't get them out of my thoughts" she told him. "Me either hon, I have done nothing but think of them and some how wonder if they had something to do with us being here this weekend". "I know it sounds far fetched and way out there" he said, "but, I just can't help it". She assured her husband that it wasn't that "far out there" after all, because, she too had thoughts that these two lovers had somehow brought them to Madison County. With that he took her in his arms, kissed her good morning and told her that he loved her very much. She too said she loved him and scampered out of bed to take her shower. With her shower done, hair and makeup to go, Ken gave her a playful swat on the bottom and told her that if she didn't hurry up, they would miss breakfast and have to settle for lunch instead. "Yeah,

yeah, I know, I know" was her response. "Don't you want me to look good though" she asked? He assured her that she always looked good to him even without makeup and her hair done. She hurried to finish and out the door to breakfast they went. "The diner again" Ken asked her? "Of course" she said, "where else"? He agreed with his wife, the diner did feel familiar and comfortable to them both already. He couldn't think of anywhere else they would rather go.

"Good morning" was the greeting as they walked through the door, waves from the locals and greetings made them feel even more at home. They smiled and waved and went to the booth they had the night before, where they learned of the story of Robert and Francesca. "Look, our booth" Nikki said as they slid in and picked up the menu. "This must be our waitress' day off" she said as they both looked around for their favorite waitress. Ken just nodded in agreement and looked at his menu. They quickly ordered and waited for their meal to arrive. They ate quickly, left a tip, and Ken went to the counter to pay the bill as Nikki got things together and ready to leave. Goodbyes were said as they walked out the door and headed for the library. They just had to find that book by Robert, they just had to they both thought.

The library was rather easy to find, and, was again, like all other places they had seen in this town, like stepping back in time. They approached the front desk and found the librarian busily checking in books and cataloging them. She looked up over the top of her tiny glasses at the couple and asked if she could help them. Nikki told her they would like to know if the book by Robert, that Francesca's children had donated was in or not. Curiously the tiny woman looked at them and said that they must have been told the story of Robert and Francesca, "that's the only reason anyone would ask for that old thing" she told them. Ken smiled a sheepish smile and said, "you got us, guilty as charged". The woman led them to an area dedicated to local writers and artists in the library, and told them that she was sure it was in. "You will find it in this area" they were told as they started their search for the book. "I found it" Nikki yelled as she jumped up and down. The librarian poked her head around the corner and quickly shushed her. Like a child caught in a cookie jar, Nikki whispered "I'm sorry". They sat at a table, opened the book and tried to see if any of the pictures looked familiar to them, from what they had already seen of the area. "Anything we recognize we will go to first, anything we don't, we will just have to start asking questions and lots of them" Ken told her. She agreed with some hesitation, but knew he was right. "Some of these places we may never find" she said. "I know honey, but, we will try our best to find them all if we can". "Why don't we copy off the pictures and take them with us, maybe with copies and our questions, we can put some pieces of this puzzle in place" he told her. "That's a great idea, why didn't I think of it" she asked? "You would have if I had given you enough time" he assured her and off to the copy machine they headed.

With the copies of pictures in hand they headed back to the front desk and the little lady behind it. "Could you tell us, by chance, where any of these places are located" Ken asked? She looked up at them and pushed her glasses firmly back on her face and picked up the pictures. "Some of these will be very easy for me to identify, while others, I have to tell you both now, I have no idea where they were taken". She quickly identified the ones she could and gave them directions to the spots. The ones she was unsure of, or, had no idea of where they were taken, were put into another pile and set aside. "Most of these that I recognize" she told them, "are either of the Roseman or Holliwell bridges". "These pictures of the woman standing on the bridge are of Francesca herself" she told them. She was a very pretty lady they thought as they looked at the pictures. She appeared to be tall for a woman, slender build, long auburn hair with red highlights and striking dark eyes. "She's pretty" Nikki said to Ken as they inspected the picture. Sorting through the photos, the tiny lady came upon the last few. "These are pictures of Francesca's house, I know where that is" she told them. With directions to the house, and, pictures identified that could be identified, complete with directions to each, they set off on their journey. On their way out of the library they noticed the time, it was still early, only around 9:30 in the morning.

Making a final check of the car for film, camera, maps and directions to all of the bridges and places the librarian had identified, they were off. The first stop would be the Cutler-Donahoe bridge located right in the city park in Winterset. Pictures were taken and poses were struck as Nikki stood by the opening and Ken snapped away. Next they decided to try to find the house Francesca lived in, as it was out in the country and they wanted to go early. The directions they were given were precise and accurate and they soon found themselves outside the gate that led to the house.

Chapter 6

Stopping the car at the side of the road and getting out to have a look around, they soon spotted a man on a tractor in the field beside the property. Ken walked to the fence line and the man pulled the tractor up and got off with a hearty Hi. Ken told him that they were curious about the house from the story they heard in town about Francesca and Robert. The man smiled and said "we get that a lot of that out here" and explained to Ken that he just leased the land for farming and that the house had been empty for some time now. "Her daughter used to stay there for a while after her Mom died, but, even she moved away again and the house has set empty ever since". Ken asked if there would be any way to get in touch with someone to ask permission to go in and see the house. The man just shook his head no and said that he couldn't think of anyone that is still around these parts that could do that. With hope starting to fade quickly, Ken thanked the man for his time and looked toward the car shaking his head no. The farmer could see the disappointment on the face of the woman in the car and stopped Ken. "I'll tell you what" the man said, "as long as you just go in and look around and take a few pictures, I can't see where anyone would mind". "You folks are probably one of the very few that even ask permission and I will be here most of the day anyway if anyone stops and says anything to you". "Just tell them that Jack said it would be ok". Ken shook the man's hand vigorously and thanked him profusely and ran back to the car. "You won't believe this" he told Nikki. "He said we could go in and take some pictures and look around". "He said that he will be here all day working the field and if anyone stops us, we are to tell them Jack said it's ok". She shrieked with delight.

The driveway to the house was long and dusty, as it was gravel. Of course out in the country like this, all roads seem to be gravel. As they pulled up in front of the house they first noticed that the house was much larger than it first appeared from the road. It was tattered and ran down from weather and age and was much in need of some tender loving care and help. "This could be a beautiful old house if someone took the time to fix it up and take care of it" Ken told his wife. She was mesmerized by the house, it was as if Francesca herself were on the porch, beckoning Nikki in for a fresh glass of tea.

27

Shaking her head to clear her thoughts, she asked Kenny "did you say something dear"? He just laughed and told her again that it could be a great old house if cleaned and fixed up. She just shook her head yes and walked toward the front door. Peering through the windows, in the front of the old house, it was plain to see that it was at one time a grand old home. Lots of natural woodwork and natural wood floors flowed throughout the house. Without thought Nikki turned the handle and the door swung open. "Could it have been unlocked all these years" she asked Ken? Directly inside the front door was a hallway. With rooms on the left and right and a staircase to the upstairs in front and to the right of them, they wandered a little further into the house. The door on the left led to what appeared to have been either an office of some kind, or, a den. They came to that conclusion with the broken remnants of furniture scattered about the room. The room directly to the right seemed to be an old parlor of some kind complete with fireplace. Further down the hallway and to the left of the bottom of the staircase was another room with a fireplace and an old broken TV it in. This could have been the living room from the looks of things they thought. To the right of the bottom of the stairway was another door leading to what looked like a formal dining room with yet another fireplace and built in china cabinets. To the left was a wide, open doorway leading to the old country kitchen that was always the heart of most of these old homes. Complete with lots of cabinet and counter space. Cobwebs and dirt were everywhere as most of the windows were either broken or had holes in them from what looked like rocks thrown at them by local kids out for a night of mischief in the country. "It's a shame to see an old house like this go to waste" Nikki said. Ken quickly agreed with her, "someone needs to find these old places and clean and fix them up and put people in them". "It's just a shame to see things like this" he said.

The kitchen had 3 doors leading to the outside, one on the left and right and one straight through and out the back. The door to the left led to a big old porch and the driveway, the door to the right led out to a screen- covered porch that led to the windmill and what looked like it must have been a garden area at one time. The door out the back opened to the back of the house and the driveway that led out behind the house to the barn area. This room also appeared to be a combination mud room and laundry room as an old laundry sink was mounted in the corner. "It's really too bad that they didn't find someone to take the old place over" Ken told her. They walked about the yard snapping pictures of the yard and house. Back inside Nikki took pictures of every room and even went upstairs to find the area very well preserved under the circumstances. While touring the inside of the house they both felt as though they weren't alone. A feeling they couldn't explain or shake, it was though someone was right there beside them with every step. "You aren't going to believe this" Ken started to say and before he could get the words formed, she finished his sentence, "someone is here with us" she said. They just looked at each other in total awe and bewilderment. Now how could that be he thought, neither one of them believed in ghosts or spirits, or things like that, but yet, it was an unmistakable feeling that they were definitely not alone in this house.

Back in the front yard of the home, they walked and looked at the neglected flower gardens that were still evident after all this time. A tire swing still hanging in the tree in the front of the house was gently swinging with the early morning breeze. It appeared as though someone was gently and lazily swinging back and forth on a lazy summer morning. Ken was more interested in the structure of the old house, something they should have thought about and checked on before they entered the old place. He found it to be in remarkable shape for the years it had set empty. Even the roof was in amazingly good condition, it was in dire need of a fresh layer of shingles, but, other than that, appeared to be in very sound shape. Several out buildings scattered the lay of the land behind the house, most falling apart from age and rot. An old corn crib sat off to one side and had been reduced to nothing but a roof and concrete base, not sure whether decay and old age was the culprit or maybe the victim of a sudden storm that Iowa is so famous for. None the less, it lost the fight and was reduced to nothing but the base and roof and looked so defeated and lonely over there in the corner.

Back inside, they ventured up the stairs. At the top was a landing with doors to the right and left and a hallway running along the wall to the left which led to more rooms. The door to the left seemed to be the master bedroom. An old Queen size mattress and box springs still lay atop a broken heap of wood that they could only assume would have been, at one time, the frame. The room to the right must have been one of her children's rooms as it too had a torn and tattered old mattress and other remains strewn about that would lead one to believe it might have belonged to her daughter at one time. Straight ahead and still to the right was yet another room with a torn old heap of a mattress that would suggest the other child's room, the son they deduced. Another room was directly in front of them and had an old sewing machine tossed in a corner, again suggesting this room must have been an old sewing room. They both looked in the room as if in a trance and could almost envision Francesca sitting at her machine mending old torn clothes. To the right was yet another room, walking through the door into the room they noticed another door to the left. It was very hard to imagine what this room was used for as the door to the left led to a bathroom. In the right corner of this mystery room was a door that led to a back stairway to the kitchen.

The bathroom still had the old cast iron, claw foot tub along one wall with an old shower head that reminded one of a ripe sunflower. The head was big and the neck bent as from the weight of the seeds in the center of the sunflower. Complete with an old circular shower curtain that when closed barely had enough room to conceal one average sized adult. The huge old cask iron sink was mounted in the corner on the wall opposite the tub and the stool hid behind the door as it opened into the room. Along the back wall of the room was another door that led to another floor. The attic room appeared to be another bedroom or possibly servants quarters in the old homes heyday. Gingerly descending the back stairway to the kitchen one could almost hear the banging of pots and clinking of spoons against the pots as Francesca busily prepared dinner for her and Robert. If you closed your eyes and concentrated the couple could swear they smelled chicken frying and freshly picked vegtables. Shaking their heads as if to clear their minds, they step into the kitchen once again. As they stood there in the middle of the kitchen they still could swear they were being followed from room to room by someone, but, they both knew in fact that they were alone in the house. Or were they?

With pictures taken of every room, and, what was left of the grounds and out buildings they started back to the car. As Ken reached to open the passenger door for his wife, they both unmistakably heard the old screen door slam shut. They both jerked around and looked in that direction to see nothing. There was no wind to speak of, a gentle summer breeze was blowing, but they both knew it wasn't enough to blow the old door open and slam it shut. Nikki looked at Ken and said it was time they left, he agreed and got in the car and drove back out the lane to the gate. As they turned on to the road, they again saw the kind old farmer that let them share even a few moments with Robert and Francesca. They waved as they passed him and heard him shout "come back anytime". Ken looked over at his wife and without saying a word they joined hands and rode along in silence for a while. Neither really knowing what to say, or think at this point. It was Nikki that broke the silence, "where to next hon"? It wasn't anything profound or brilliant but at this point it was all she could muster. Ken pulled the car to the shoulder of the road, put the car in park, turned to his wife, took her hands in his and looked deep into her crystal blue eyes. "Nikki, I know what I am about to say may sound crazy and entirely ludicrous, but, I don't want to leave and go home until we retrace the steps of Robert and Francesca as close and completely as we can". Fighting back tears, she could only say, "I was hoping you would feel that way, me too". Looks like we might be here more than a couple of days Ken told her. "I know honey" she said, "I know". "Let's stop by the room and lay out our plan" Ken told her, she nodded in agreement and off they went.

K. F. Coffman

Chapter 7

Back in the comfort of the room, they both sat on the bed and just held each other for a few moments. "Ken, I can't explain what happened back there in that house" she said. "I can't either, but, we both know that we weren't alone babe". What exactly had happened was about as unclear as what had drawn them to this area in the first place. The one thing they did agree on was they weren't about to leave until they found out, and, somehow revisit as many of the spots Robert and Francesca held secret for all these years. Could it somehow be that these two lovers, destined to love so completely and absolutely, have somehow brought this couple full of doubts and uncertainty here to show them there is no such thing as a hurdle too large to overcome? It sounds like a plot from a low budget sci-fi movie and yet here they were, right in the middle of it. One thing was certain, they were both determined to see this thing through to the very end, no matter where that might lead them or what they might discover along the way. They were in this together.

As they laid out the copies of the pictures from Roberts book on the bed and tried to arrange them in some kind of order, they took out maps they had accumulated along the way and mapped out their next move. From what we know to be accurate and precise directions, from more than one person we have spoken to, the next logical move seems to be the Holliwell bridge. From what we have been able to piece together Robert and Francesca met at the house. We have been there and know that something is definitely driving us on. From what we have learned, they went to the Roseman bridge next, then back to the house. I would like to leave the Roseman for the last stop Ken said. Nikki wholeheartedly agreed, there was something almost spiritual about the bridge that stands guard over them as a final resting place she said. We know also that their next meeting seemed to be at the Holliwell bridge, and, that is where Robert first captured the images of Francesca on film. Again they agreed and decided that the Holliwell would be the next stop, but, where to from there? According to what we know now, they went back to the house and then to various spots in the county that are as yet unidentified. That must be these pictures of her in what looks like a park or pasture of some kind.

33

That would be the hardest part of their search they thought. Like finding the proverbial needle in the haystack. They picked up their maps and pictures and headed for the door. The drive to the Holliwell bridge was quiet and enjoyable as they sang along to songs on the radio they knew, and laughed and held hands. Ken couldn't remember the last time she held him like this, it seemed that she would never let go and it felt good, it felt right. As if something terribly wrong was suddenly being made right, he just knew deep in his heart that this trip was going to save them. It already seemed to have shown them both the way back to each other in just a day and a half and they had just begun their journey. They both knew they had a love that could, and has, stayed the test of time. It was one that would and could last through the unimaginable and somehow bring them even closer. It seemed that what would doom most relationships only made them stronger and more determined to overcome. What would poison most, theirs seemed to thrive on. That's why Ken knew that he just had to get her away this weekend, and, this place was the only place they could again find "them".

The Holliwell bridge came into view as they traveled the winding hilly gravel road. Tucked away amidst the trees and overgrowth the old bridge spanned a bubbling creek, the water below sparkling like tiny diamonds shining in the brilliant afternoon sun. They parked the car and walked slowly toward the bridge, again having it all to themselves. As they strolled from one side to the other they looked at the pictures they had copied from the book and recognized the spot that Francesca stood and had her picture snapped by Robert. "She was standing in that very spot" he told his wife. "Look, you can see the railing and the markings on the wood behind her". Francesca stood in this very spot and posed unexpectedly for her new love, years before, and now Nikki was standing there just as she had. "I'll take a picture of you just like he did, give me a pose" he told her. As Nikki tucked her hands behind her, as Francesca had so many years ago, Ken focused the camera. Looking through the viewfinder of the camera trying to get just the right pose, Ken turned white as a sheet and dropped the camera. Nikki rushed over to his side, with fear and worry in her eyes, she wrapped her arms around him to steady him and asked if it was his back. He just stuttered and said he needed to sit down for a minute. Afraid that he may have overdone it the last couple of days, she walked with him to the edge of the bridge and they sat on the bank. "Are you ok" she asked with definite concern in her voice?

"You won't believe what I am about to say Nikki" he started. "Try me love" she responded, "what is it, what's wrong, what happened"? "When I looked through the viewfinder of the camera and tried to focus on you, I..I...I" he stammered, "I saw Francesca standing there behind you". "I know there is no conceivable way on Gods green earth that this could happen, but it did" he told her. As far fetched as it sounded Nikki believed him. "You know, I believe you" she said, "as a matter of fact I felt as though I wasn't alone just then". "The hair on the back of my neck stood up and I felt a chill go straight through me, I mean clear to the bone kind of chill Ken". How in the world could this be happening they thought as they sat on the river bank and just held each other? Somehow, someway, something or someone was trying to reach these two lovers and help them find their way back to a love that is ever lasting and true. Something they had lost sight of lately, as they had been too wrapped up in their problems to see the toll it was taking on the relationship. They gathered their thoughts and once again Nikki posed at the opening of the bridge and Ken took several snapshots of his beautiful wife. They walked hand in hand back to the car and sat in silence for a few minutes. Finally Ken spoke up and suggested they drive over to the Imes bridge as it didn't have anything to do with Robert and Francesca, as far as they knew. Nikki agreed and scooted close to him, curling up next to her husband as they drove along. This is something she hadn't done in years she thought and it felt good, it just felt like the only place in the world she felt safe and whole right now. Ken put an arm around his wife and pulled her close as they drove along to see the fifth of the six bridges.

The Imes bridge was located on the eastern edge of a small town called St. Charles. The bridge had been moved to this spot and a small park created for people to stop, photograph and enjoy the bridge. Upon reading the information they had on the old bridge they learned that the Imes was the oldest of the remaining six bridges. Built in 1870 and one of only two of the remaining six bridges that have a sloped roof. The other four have flat roofs. It was like all the others, renovated and set in a quaint little setting that reminded one of days gone by. They walked through the bridge and marveled at the soundness of the construction and the peaceful and easiness the bridge made one feel. It was as though walking through these old bridges took your cares and worries away and left you relaxed and be at ease. It was almost therapeutic they thought. Again the camera was out and pictures were snapped and poses were struck. This time though, unlike all the others, they weren't alone. Several other people were there and one couple was even eating a late lunch inside the bridge. Ken and Nikki stopped and talked to them and found they were here from Arizona, another couple they spoke to was from Kansas. "Seems that these old bridges draw people from all over" Ken said. "Looks like it" she responded. They spent some time just relaxing and putting Robert and Francesca behind them for the moment. They felt they had experienced enough of the unexplainable for the moment and just wanted to revel in the moment. With that, Ken asked if she wanted to drive back to Winterset and get a late lunch. She agreed and were once again on the road.

Walking into the diner, they felt like returning home in some strange way. They were again greeted by hello's and waves and their favorite booth was empty. They slid in and picked up menus. Without even looking up from their menus the waitress set glasses of water before them and said "I'll be back in a bit". They just nodded and were lost, deep in thought. How could any of this be happening? Ken was a fairly well educated person with a very open mind to things that had no explanation or reasoning for them, but, even this was beginning to bewilder him. Nikki, like her husband, had a very open mind to things that no one could explain, but, she too had some trouble grasping this. They finally shook it off and concentrated on the menu in front of them, finally deciding on lunch, they looked up to find the kind old waitress they had spoke to the night before taking their order. "You two look like you've just seen a ghost" she said as she readied to take their order. "You wouldn't believe me if we told you" was Kens reply. "Believe it or not, you wouldn't be the first to tell me they saw or heard something strange" the lady told them. With orders placed and drinks in hand, they sat back in their booth and tried to understand just what had happened to them this morning.

They ate lunch for the most part in silence, small talk about what they would do next or see next was the only thing that broke that silence. After their meal they decided to treat themselves to dessert and ordered fresh baked pie. The kind old waitress strolled over and asked if she could once again join them, they agreed. Sitting and explaining to the woman what they had heard and seen made them feel more than a little squeamish, it made them feel as though they were losing touch with reality. She assured them that they weren't the first that had experienced something like this and probably wouldn't be the last. In some strange way just talking about it with this woman seemed to help. She asked if they found the book in the library and they nodded yes. Ken did ask the lady if she might be able to help them locate a couple of spots that the librarian didn't recognize. "I'll try my best" she said as they took the pictures out and spread them on the table top. They showed her the ones that had been identified, and, the spots they had already visited. "These shots of this old stone bridge and park, or pasture, are what seems to elude everyone" Ken told her. "Seems they had some sort of outing there and no one we have spoken to seems to know where it could be". As if in some deep trance the old woman closed her eyes and was lost in thought. As if jabbed with a needle or something, the woman's eyes opened wide and she jerked to face them. "I know someone that might just be able to help you locate this spot" she told them. She slid out of the booth, walked toward the back of the diner and disappeared through a doorway. Ken and Nikki could only look at each other in total disbelief.

What seemed like an eternity later, actually it was only a few minutes, the woman returned to their table. She had a smile from ear to ear and was practically beaming. "I found someone for you to talk to that can help fill in a lot of blanks you still have" she told them. "I didn't offer the information before because I wasn't sure if this person would feel comfortable talking to you about this". "She agreed that she will help in any way she can with your quest". They both nearly jumped from the booth and it was Ken that put his arms around the old woman and hugged her. "Thank you so much for all the help" he told her, Nikki too gave her a big hug before they paid the check and left the diner. The lady had given Ken a folded piece of paper with the name Lucy on it and a phone number. They went back to their room so they could speak in private and write down as much as this Lucy person could tell them, they didn't want to miss a thing.

Chapter 8

Ken picked up the phone and with shaky hands dialed the number on the scrap of paper the waitress had handed him. It was obvious he was nervous and he couldn't really explain why. The phone rang several times and he was about to hang up and try again later when a frail, shaky little voice answered and just said hello. He gave Nikki the thumbs up sign indicating that he had gotten through to someone. "Hello, is Lucy there" was all he could muster, any other words just seemed to stick in his throat. "This is Lucy" the faint little voice answered, "can I help you"? Ken proceeded to explain that they got her number from the waitress at the diner and was told to call. She acknowledged giving her permission for the woman to pass her number on as they talked. Ken found much to his surprise that Lucy too lived on a small farm outside town, not far from Francesca's old run down home. She gave him directions to her home and told him that if they were looking for information, she would be happy to meet them at her house as she doesn't get out much anymore. He understood and agreed to come to her and told her he and his wife would be there shortly. Directions were given and they exchanged goodbyes and the couple hurriedly grabbed what they thought they needed and headed out the door. "So, what did she say" asked Nikki? He explained that she didn't really say much over the phone but agreed to meet them and tell them what she knew. They could hardly wait.

The afternoon was beginning to give way to early dusk and a noticeable haze was hoovering just above the tops of the rows of corn standing at full attention in the fields. Like row after row of finely trained soldiers standing at attention awaiting their orders to march off to battle. Rays of sunlight beamed through some high cumulus clouds that had formed during the day and gave the appearance of stairways to heaven. It was a picture perfect evening for a drive in the country, the land green and lush and the reds and oranges of the pending sunset softly brushing the horizon, it was beautiful they thought. They followed the directions to the tiny farm to the letter and soon found themselves turning into a short drive leading to a small white frame house. The house was small but attractive with Wedgewood Blue shutters and trim and a freshly mowed and well kept yard. Small flower beds scattered about were in full bloom and several chairs sat on the large front porch. Quite the opposite of Francesca's house which sat far back from the road and was somewhat concealed by trees, Lucy's home was close to the road and very visible. As they approached the house they noticed a tiny, frail white-haired old woman rocking gently in a rocker placed in a corner of the porch. Ken stepped up and gently asked if she might be Lucy? The tiny woman gave a beaming smile and just said yes. "Welcome to my home, I don't get many visitors here" she exclaimed. "It's our pleasure Ma'am" Ken replied. She motioned for them to pull up chairs and asked if they would care for some fresh ice tea or something, they gladly accepted and Nikki offered to help retrieve the refreshments. With Lucy on her arm the two disappeared into the house and returned shortly with a tray. They sat and talked and soon were lost in conversation about times past, loves found and lost and had answers to most of their questions. Lucy indeed knew the secret locations of the photos that had everyone else stumped and befuddled. The couple learned that during that particular time, Lucy was involved herself with a local farmer in a torrid affair and was a marked woman by most. She felt that Francesca befriended her because they shared something that only they could understand. "We were inseparable" the tiny woman told them, but, "I didn't find out until years later about her and Robert myself". "I guess it was something she just wasn't ready to share with anyone until she wanted to" the old woman told them.

As the evening turned into night and the hours passed, they talked and laughed and the kindly old woman learned that they had come to this area to get back something they felt they had lost in their own relationship. "This area can do that for ya" she said. "There has been one other time, before this, that someone came to me for some answers about those two" she said. As they talked and told her of the unexplainable occurrences they had experienced that day the old woman just smiled and nodded. "Those two brought you here for a reason" she told them "and it will become crystal clear to you before you leave why". She gave them directions to the secret areas that the photos only hinted of and shared something else with them. "That I know of, no one has been to that place since she passed on" she started. "It was their secret place and Franny went there every year on her birthday to be as close to Robert as she could". "It was all she had left of him, it was all she had left of them and the times they spent together". "It was the one place on this earth she could go to be with him and didn't have to worry about anyone or anything spoiling it or making it sordid and dirty for her". "Can you understand that" the old woman asked with tears forming in her eyes. Ken too had tears forming in his eyes and through tear blurred eyes just took her tiny, wrinkled hand in his and knelt before her and said "yes Lucy, I do understand". He then kissed her frail hand and told her how much they enjoyed visiting with her and assured her that the location they were about to visit would be as sacred to them as it had been to Francesca and Robert. "I know it will be my dear, I know you will keep it safe" she told the big man. They helped her back into the house and said their goodbyes and asked if there was anything they could do for her before they left. All she could say was "come back again, I don't get many visitors out here anymore, since Franny died". They promised her they would return and closed the door behind them. "You know, I plan on keeping that promise" he told Nikki as they walked to the car. "You better, I plan on making you keep it too" she replied.

They sat close and held hands on the return trip to town. Deciding it was long past time to eat, they spotted a local pizza shop and pulled in. They ordered and ate and without saying a single word could tell that this trip had already brought something back that they thought was lost. They finished dinner and left for their motel. On the way back to the room, they turned to each other and without a word, both nodded. He quickly turned the car around and drove back out toward the house that Francesca and Robert had found a love so strong, so pure and rare, that not even death could deny it. The front of the old house was illuminated by an almost full moon. The night sky was bright and stars were twinkling like diamonds scattered on black velvet. They turned to each other and kissed, a long, deep, passionate kiss you feel to your very being. "You know you are the most important thing in my life" he told her. With tears starting to build, she could only shake her head and say "I know". They got out of the car, sat on the hood and stared at the house. Suddenly they both turned to each other in total disbelief. "You do see that right" Nikki asked? Ken could feel that she was trembling, he held her even closer and said "yes baby, I see it". Her head resting on his shoulder and safe in his arms, they watched the house and saw the distinct image of two people, they appeared to be dancing as candles flickered and soft jazz music played. They just smiled at each other, kissed again and Ken said, "let's give them some privacy". They drove back to the motel tightly clinging to each other.

Nikki opened the door of their room and stepped inside, Ken followed close behind. They closed the door and he once again took his wife in his arms and pulled her gently to him. He kissed her again, this time with such passion they swore sparks flew. They made their way to the bed and she sat on the edge. He went to his bag, reached in and withdrew about half a dozen candles. He had come prepared, praying for a moment exactly like this, it looked as if his prayers were being answered. He lit the candles and found a station on the radio with soft rock music playing. He moved back to were Nikki sat and slowly went down to his knees in front of her. He took her hands in his and again found himself lost in those beautiful blue eyes of hers. As he slowly undressed her, he kissed every inch of skin as it was exposed. Soon they were in bed making love like it was their first time. It was so passionate and beautiful that night, almost as if someone else were possessing their bodies. Their hearts and souls truly became one that night. It was as though they weren't two separate people anymore, but one. One heart beating for two, one breath breathing for two, one soul to share for the rest of their lives. It was so intense and beautiful, breath taking and earth shattering at the same time. Their lips met, their fingers entwined, their bodies melded into one being that night. It was true, that night after 25 years of marriage, they became one heart, one soul, one being and they loved the feeling. Soon they fell fast asleep wrapped in each others arms and lost in each others souls. It was one of the most peaceful and rewarding sleeps they had ever experienced.

Chapter 9

The morning sun pouring through the small opening between the blinds and the sound of birds singing their morning serenade woke them. They smiled and again Ken looked deep into her eyes and kissed her good morning, telling her how very much he loved her. Her mind still reeling from the night before and her knees more than a little weak, she held her husband close and said "I love you to Ken". "I'm so glad we came here" she told him. They quickly showered and packed as this would be the day they would return home. "One last breakfast at the diner" he asked as they checked and double checked the room to make sure they weren't forgetting anything. "Yes, of course" she replied as they locked the door and returned the key to the front desk. The bubbly young woman at the front desk checked them out and said she hoped they had an enjoyable stay. They turned and looked at each other and broke out laughing hysterically. If only she knew they thought as they told her yes and went to the car. Arm in arm, they practically skipped to the car and got in. "To the diner" Ken said as he pointed in the general direction of the small café they found 3 days ago. "Yes" she shrieked as the car backed out and pulled onto the street and headed toward the town square and the diner.

Inside the diner they once again found their booth available and the waitress that had helped them so many times, in so many ways there also. She waved enthusiastically as they entered and met them at their booth with glasses of water and menus. "You are just glowing" she told Nikki. "Anything you can share" she asked? Nikki blushed and giggled and the lady smiled and just said, "enough said my dear". "The usual" she asked as they glanced at their menus. "Sure, why not" they replied and she was off to place their order and return with coffee pot in hand. "Going home today" she asked as she poured fresh coffee for them. "Yes, unfortunately" Ken said. They told her they wished they had more time but needed to get back to kids, grandchildren and pets. She smiled and nodded and said she understood. They assured her that they would be back though. As they sat enjoying breakfast Nikki took out a small piece of paper and wrote their address on it. They finished, left a tip and as Ken went to pay the bill, Nikki went over to the old woman and handed her the paper and hugged her and thanked her for everything. As they left waves and goodbyes were exchanged with everyone in the diner and they were once again off. Before they left Ken asked the cashier if there was a florist in town open on Sunday? The supermarket was the only place anyone could think of that would have flowers for sale on Sunday. "Next stop the supermarket" he told Nikki as they made their way to the car. "Why do you need flowers" she asked? "You'll see" is all he would say as he pulled into a parking spot. "I'll be right back" he said as he exited the car and went inside. He returned a few minutes later with a large bag and a smile.

Following Lucy's directions they found the old stone bridge that spanned an old dried up creek bed. Crossing it led to the secluded spot Francesca and Robert shared so many years before. Their private place to be away from the world and share a love so rare that few ever find anything like it while others believe it doesn't exist at all. They snapped photos of the bridge, the clearing just beyond, and vowed never to share these photos with anyone but themselves. It would remain Francesca and Robert's secret, shared only with Lucy and now them. They sat and enjoyed the uninterrupted peace and tranquility that this sacred place offered for a while. Their final destination on a journey to find themselves that started 3 days ago, would be the Roseman bridge. The place where it all began and ended for these lovers, starting with a woman showing a stranger some kindness and directions and ending with the two of them to be together for all eternity. A luxury they never got to experience while they were alive but would share forever in the ever after. This would be the fitting end to their journey also Ken and Nikki thought. What could be more fitting, what could be more right? "I'll be right back" Ken said as he went toward the car. He reached inside and took something out of the bag he got from the supermarket. Nikki could see if was an arrangement of flowers. They laid the flowers in the clearing as if to pay their respects to the couple and turned to leave. "I understand now why you wanted flowers" she said as they got in the car and headed toward the Roseman bridge. It just seemed fitting he said as they drove along, she quickly agreed and they drove on.

It was almost noon by the time they reached their last stop, the Roseman bridge. The noon sun directly overhead almost gave the illusion of a heavenly glow to the old bridge. It was solemn and peaceful and they again had the bridge to themselves. For some unexplainable reason they seemed to have most of the bridges to themselves this weekend and for that they were somewhat thankful. Ken reached in and grabbed the bag from the supermarket and took it with them this time. They walked from one side to the other through the bridge listening to the Middle River lazily flowing beneath them. It was no wonder they found this to be the perfect place to spend all eternity with each other, after all, this seemed like heaven to Ken and Nikki. Wild flowers lining the banks on both sides, the Middle River winding and flowing gently and lazily along with the backdrop of crystal clear blue skies as far as one could see, this had to be what heaven would look like they thought. Nikki posed as more pictures were taken, and, once again, Ken could swear he saw someone or something behind Nikki when he looked through the viewfinder. This time he wasn't alarmed or frightened, he found himself to be humbled and at peace instead. Lowering the camera a bit he said "I don't think you are alone anymore". "I feel them to" Nikki added and she smiled. She too felt a certain peace and harmony deep within herself and felt that this was the perfect ending to a weekend journey she would never forget. He again raised the camera and could swear he saw a couple standing behind his wife. He took the picture and smiled. He and Nikki threw the flowers off the sides of the bridge in memory of two people that lived before them yet somehow found it possible to lead them here and help them find something they felt was lost.

As they walked through the bridge to the car they could swear they heard the distinct clicking of a camera. They looked at each other and smiled as they wrapped their arms around each others waist and continued through the bridge. Just before reaching the other side they found these words written on the wall of the majestic old bridge. "This kind of certainty comes but once in a lifetime". Not knowing if this was something someone copied from a quote somewhere, or whether it was something Robert might have told Francesca all those years ago, of one thing they both were certain. Truer words could never have been spoken for they had found that very certainty that very weekend. As they drove north to the interstate to finish their homeward trek, they were very certain indeed of several things. They both knew that they would leave a part of them with Robert and Francesca right there in Madison County. They knew that they had found something that weekend they never realized they had before. Whether it was something they felt they lost along the way and found in this mystical, magical place, or, something they really never had before and discovered it for the first time this weekend, one thing was for sure. They were leaving with much more than they arrived with and they knew now that it would be with them forever. They found that taking things for granted isn't always the best way to do things, follow your heart. They did this weekend, and, they found an inner peace and happiness that few ever find. And they knew that they would return, that was a promise that they made each other at the Roseman bridge and didn't intend on breaking it.

They pulled back onto the Interstate they had exited just 3 short days ago. They came to this area full of doubt in each other and themselves, worry, and a bit of disbelief in just where they were headed as a couple. They left full of love for one another, and, an understanding of what that love meant. Something most only dream of finding. It was true what they say about this area bringing people together, they found that out first hand this weekend. As they drove along, hand in hand, they felt an inner peace that words could not describe. Without ever saying a word they both were silently planning their return. That was the one thing they both agreed on, they were destined to return to this beautiful, captivating place, and, it would be soon. Nikki leaned over and gently kissed her husband on the cheek and said "thank you my love". "What was that for" he asked? "For a time in my life that I will never forget" she said. "I don't think either of us will ever forget it babe" he replied.

Chapter 10

The trip home seemed to pass quickly and they really didn't want to go back just yet. "I have an idea" Ken said. "What's that" Nikki asked? The exit is just ahead to that town you originally thought we were going to. "Want to stop and check out all the little shops" he asked? She grinned from ear to ear and told him that sounded like a good idea to her. "Did you even have to ask if I wanted to shop" she asked as they exited the Interstate. "I've said it before and I'll say it again" he told her, "when will I ever learn"? They laughed and headed down the main street of the little town. Lining the street on both sides were antique and specialty shops and a few local eateries. They found a parking spot at one end of the street and decided to walk up one side, back down the other and back to the car.

As they strolled from shop to shop, looking for nothing in particular, they saw old dishes, furniture and nick-nacks and found themselves saying how that would look good in the kitchen or living room of Francesca's old home. They just couldn't help themselves it seemed, their thoughts seemed to return to the house and that area without even realizing it. They laughed and shook their heads and moved on, to the next shop. They paused in front of one of the quaint little cafes the town sported and realized they hadn't had lunch yet. They found themselves both very hungry and decided to have a late lunch after all. The inside was decorated with antique furniture from the Victorian era and was quite appealing. They soon found a place to set and ordered. "I sure miss the diner" Nikki said. Ken laughed and said he too missed the place. It had become a familiar old friend to them in a very short time and they truly missed not having lunch there. They finished their meal, paid the check and continued their shopping.

With only two small shops left, Ken asked if she wanted to go in and check them out or just leave now. Nikki was a bit reluctant, but, said she wanted to check out the last shops and then they would leave. They entered the first and found nothing that caught their attention. The last shop was about to close as they entered the front door. "We will be closing in a short time" the clerk told them as they walked about the store. They assured her that they would leave shortly and continued their tour of the old store. As they were about to leave, Ken spotted some racks lined with old toys in the corner and wandered over to look. He shook his head in disbelief and told Nikki to come over and look at something. "Do you still have the copies of those pictures from Roberts book in your purse" he asked? "Yeah I do, but why" she asked in return? "Let me see them please" he told her as she reached in her bag to retrieve them. "Here they are" she said as she handed them to him. As Ken flipped through the pictures she asked if he was looking for one in particular. He told her he was looking for the picture of Roberts truck. Finally finding it, he looked at her and their mouths both dropped open. It was an old 1960's model GMC truck and there on the toy rack was a metal die cast model of the same truck. It was even green like Roberts. They immediately bought the tiny toy truck and thanked the clerk as they left. "Find something special" the clerk asked as they paid for their new find? They smiled at each other and just told her that she had no idea of the treasure they had just found. Waving goodbye and leaving the store they walked back to their car arm in arm. "Home James" Nikki said as they backed out onto the street. They both laughed and continued homeward. It had been an unforgettable weekend Ken thought, and, he pulled it off without her knowing a thing. He was very proud of himself, very proud indeed.

Pulling into the drive at home they were greeted by the yapping and barking of their dog. As they opened the door they were almost bowled over by the anxious little critter. Ken stooped and picked up his little friend and hugged him. I guess we were missed he told Nikki as they carried in bags and treasures found along the way. They hurriedly unpacked and put dirty clothes in the laundry then sat down in time to catch the local news on TV. They both agreed to relax and wait for Jr to come home and see if he wanted to go out for a late dinner with them and hear all about their adventure. Just then the phone rang, it was their son Will calling from boot camp. "Boy that was timing" Nikki said as she started telling their youngest all about the fantastic time they had this last weekend. Handing the phone to Ken, his son greeted him with a happy birthday Dad. "I would say that I'm sorry I missed it, but, it doesn't sound like I need to" Will told his father. "No son, you don't need to at all, but, I would say that your Mom and I missed you though" Ken told his son. "Good" Will said, "I was beginning to think that you didn't even notice that I was gone". "Now how could we ever do that" Ken asked? They talked and laughed and found him to be good and having a great time. They would see him soon as they were traveling down to see him graduate boot camp in just a few short weeks. They said their goodbyes and told him they would see him soon and hung up the phone. That was the ending to a great weekend he told Nikki, hearing from Will. She agreed as Ken took her in his arms and kissed her. "Have I told you how much I love you today" he asked? "Yes you have my dear, but feel free to tell me again, I could never get tired of hearing it". They kissed again, passionately as their son Jr walked through the door.

"Yuck, stop that" he yelled as his parents were wrapped in each others arms. "You two are too old to do that sort of thing" he said with a smile. "We'll never be too old son" Ken told him. Have you ate, or are you waiting to see if we were home and what we made you for dinner Ken asked? "What do you think Dad" Jr said? Ken just looked at Nikki and said "it figures, we have to feed him again". Jr unpacked and joined them in the car to go have dinner. "So, how was your trip" their son asked? "It was great" they chimed together and laughed. "Sheesh" was his only response. "You two sure act different, anything happen" he asked? They just looked at each other and broke out in an uncontrollable laugh. "Nothing out of the ordinary son" was all Ken could muster and they drove on.

After some serious debate over where to eat, as each had a different idea of what they wanted, an agreement was reached. They stopped, went in, and found a booth. Jr told Ken that he could set next to Nikki, "after all Dad, she is yours" he said. An issue they usually argued over. Ken decided this time he agreed with his son, "yes my boy, she is mine isn't she" he said. They made their selections and waited for the waitress to return with their meal. Jr said he wanted to hear all about their weekend and Ken told their son all about the fabulous bridges and how beautiful the area was. Nikki whispered in her husband's ear "you can leave out some of the details" and she blushed. He whispered back "I was going to love, I was going to". They sat and ate and talked about the bridges and all they had seen. Their son said he would really like to go with them if they ever went back. They assured him they would go back and he could go, they told him they thought he would really like it. They ate and laughed and enjoyed being back. After their meal they went for a short ride together and returned home. It had been a long day and Nikki had to return to work tomorrow. They settled in for the night and fell fast asleep in each others arms dreaming of their weekend and the wondrous things they had found.

Unpacking the next day Ken came across Lucy's address and decided to set down and write. He wanted to tell her that they made it home without incident and they were all fine and missed her already. He told her that they had agreed, and promised, that they would return to see her and it would be soon. He told her that they found the areas she told them about and again thanked her for all her help. "I just hope she is capable of writing back" Ken thought as he sealed the envelope. He put the letter in the mail as it hadn't been picked up yet and sorted through the mail that had came while they were gone. Bills in one pile, junk mail in another, letters from Will or family in yet another. Bills were sorted into two piles, ones they could pay now and ones they wished they could pay now. The only difference between the two was the urgency in which they needed to be paid. Junk mail was ran through the shredder and letters were opened and read. Not much of a day, but it was something to take his mind of Madison County. It was all he could think of since they returned home.

Chapter 11

A couple of weeks had passed since their return from the bridges and it was time to pack once again. This trip, unlike the last, had been planned for some time now and was one they knew they would take. They were off to see their son graduate boot camp and spend a few days with him. With bags packed and the rental car picked up, it was time to load the van for the trip. They would leave early the next morning and it would be a 2-day trip down. One that Ken really wasn't looking forward to, long trips and sitting in the car for prolonged periods made his pain almost unbearable. He wanted more than anything to see his son but wasn't jumping for joy at the idea of being in a car for 2 days.

The van loaded and packed and everyone that was going already there, they ordered pizza and made a night of movies, pizza and popcorn waiting for night to fall. Bedtime seemed to come quickly that night and they tossed and turned having trouble falling off to sleep. Like a tiny child on Christmas Eve waiting for Santa, you just can't fall asleep and when you finally do, you are up much too early waiting to wake everyone and tell them it's time. Ken was the first to wake, as he usually did, and made a fresh pot of coffee. Something he was sure everyone would need this morning. With time finally upon him to wake everyone and start chasing people in and out of the bathroom, he woke Nikki first. He thought it best to give her first shot at the bathroom and a shower as she would be doing most of the driving.

Sliding in the bed next to her, she rolled into his arms and was greeted by a smiling face and an "I love you". "Is it really time" she asked as she tried to shake off the slumber of the previous night? "Yes my love, I'm afraid it is" he told her as he rousted her from the bed. "But Daddy, I don't want to go to school" she playfully whined as she stretched and rolled to the edge of the bed. With a hearty swat on her backside he told her to get up before he woke the heathens up. With Nikki's shower out of the way, hair done and makeup on, it was time to wake his son and the rest of the traveling party. Their son, a friend of both of their boys and Wills fiancé would all be making the trip today. Of course they all whined and complained that it was much too early to get up. Ken told them to get up, use the bathroom and get in the van, he told them they could sleep on the way. Like leading zombies to nowhere they quickly used the bathroom and picked their spot in the van. "I guess that was easier than I thought" he told Nikki as he did one last look around the house to make sure they weren't forgetting anything. "We haven't left yet" she told him, "things could get interesting yet". They both laughed as Ken poured the remaining coffee into a thermos and shut and locked the door. Finally, they would be on the way, Nikki had been marking days off on the calender.

Soon they were out of town and on the road to see their son. This would be the second- best trip they had taken lately he thought as he watched out the window and watched the night skies giving way to the dawn. It would be a beautiful day he thought, hot and humid, but none the less, a beautiful day. They traveled on and one by one the weary passengers woke to ask in bewilderment "where are we"? "In a car on a trip" was Nikki's response. At times she can be a handful Ken thought. It was kind of like babysitting all three of his grandchildren at once, by himself, them on a sugar high, and no nap. He just shook his head and thought to himself, "yep, a real handful". With stops for gas and bathroom breaks and time for Ken to get out and stretch, the day was passing quickly. Before they knew it, lunch time had snuck upon them and they stopped in a rest area to eat and switch drivers for a while. With Ken now at the wheel, the trip continued. They stopped again for gas and meals and soon found themselves at their motel stop for the night.

They only took what they absolutely needed into the room that first night. They would again leave early the next morning and would see their son the next afternoon. Nikki couldn't wait. To their delight the motel had a pool and while everyone went off for a quick dip to cool off, Nikki and Ken stole a few moments together, alone. It was nice to just have a few minutes by themselves and be together. As the wayward travelers returned to the rooms, one by one, they ordered dinner from the restaurant next door and the boys ran over to pick it up. They ate, watched some TV and had some laughs. Soon it was time once again to drift off to sleep and once again leave early to finish the trip. Morning, once again, came much too early it seemed and they were again trying to get everyone in and out of bathrooms and back in the van. Once on the road, everyone slept but Ken. He had volunteered to take the first shift of driving and let everyone drift back off. Before they realized it, they were pulling into the motel that they would call home for the next 3 days. Unloading all their bags and belongings and unpacking quickly, they headed for the base to see their son for the first time in almost 7 weeks.

As they entered the gate and received directions to the area their son was staying, Nikki almost jumped out and ran the rest of the way. It was all Ken could do to restrain her. "We'll be there in a minute dear" he told her. She had waited for what feels like forever to see her baby and now that she was this close, God help anyone that got in her road now. Soon they pulled into a parking lot, found a place to park and everyone exited the car. As Nikki got out and shut the door, someone came up behind her and picked her up off the ground. Before she could say a word, she heard the words "I love you Mom". She turned to see her boy was holding his Mom and hugged him as though she would never turn him lose again. With hugs and greetings from everyone they were led into the dorm area and got to tour the place their son has called home for almost 2 months.

The graduation ceremony was a sight to behold and both Ken and Nikki were in tears the entire time. They were so very proud of their son and this was confirmation that he had grown into a man and was on his own now. Something that all parents dread seeing, their babies growing up and going their own way. Soon he would be married and starting a family of his own. Something they remember well, as if it were only yesterday. The next 2 days were spent with their son and they made every minute count. They all cried as they had to say their goodbyes and start the long trip home. The trip home was a sad one in a way, but again, one filled with pride in the accomplishments their son had already achieved. Before they knew it, they were once again home to the everyday routine or so Nikki thought.

Ken made some decisions while they were gone, and, they would be ones that he felt would change their lives forever. He only hoped it would be better changes than worse. Upon arriving home Ken found several messages on their machine from his attorney. In the last two, the attorney said it was urgent that Ken call as soon as he returned. "I wonder what that is all about" he said as he and Nikki listened to them. "Who knows" she told him, "you know how he is". "He considers it urgent if he needs your signature on a piece of paper, you know that". Ken had to agree with his wife, their attorney was known to be a bit melodramatic at times. Maybe this would again be one of those times. He would find out the next morning when he returned the call. "I guess I'll find out" he told Nikki, "I'll call him back tomorrow and see". As they settled in for the evening and watched some TV, complete with popcorn, they found themselves once again on the floor with his arms wrapped tightly around her. This seemed to be second nature lately, something they never did before they left for Madison County. Somehow it just seemed right to them now, seemed natural. They soon found it time for bed and walked hand in hand toward their room. Soon they were fast asleep, her with her headed nestled on his shoulder and he with his arms wrapped tightly around her. Again, something that seemed to be second nature to them lately.

Chapter 12

The next morning was very familiar to Ken, up around 5:00, as usual, coffee started, dog let out and ready to wake Nikki around 5:30. Inspecting the kitchen for any leftover dishes or mess, he took his first pain pill of the day. Now to wake his beautiful wife and watch her ready herself for another long, hot day at work. He stood in the doorway of their room and watched her roll and stretch, almost catlike, as she struggled to shake off the slumber of the night before. "Should I get the garden hose" he asked as she rolled to see him standing there at the door? "I don't think so" she replied. "I could always be sick today and stay home" she said as she playfully patted the empty spot in the bed beside her. "As tempting as that sounds my love, you know we can't afford the luxury" he said with a disappointing look. "I know hon, it was just a thought" she said as she once again rolled and stretched. "Shower" he sternly told her as she lazily swung her legs over the edge of the bed. "Yes master" she purred as she reached for her robe and headed for the shower. "I'll have your first cup of caffeine waiting for you dear" he yelled as he headed for the kitchen.

After getting Nikki finally out the door and on her way, Ken straightened the living room and took out what he needed for dinner that evening. Now for some coffee and local news he thought as he sat down and turned on the TV. Jr is next he thought as he watched the clock on the wall. He just couldn't shake the feeling that something big was about to happen. It had been with him since hearing his attorneys messages and the word urgent kept repeating in his mind. What in the world could be going on he wondered. He would hopefully find out around 9:00 this morning as his attorney was usually in his office by then. Noticing the time and realizing that it was already 5 minutes after eight, he rushed to his sons room and announced the time and apologized for getting him up a few minutes late. His son sat up, rubbed his eyes and yawned, and just said "huh". "Never mind" Ken told the boy, "it's time to get up bud".

Now with his son on his way to work, Nikki gone, the house straightened up and the animals fed, he decided to get on the computer and let everyone know that he hadn't fallen off the edge of the world. Time passed quickly and before he realized what time it was the phone rang. On the other end was his attorney, asking him where in the world had he been? "I went to see Will graduate boot camp, you knew that" he told the rambunctious barrister on the other end. Dave had been his attorney for what felt like forever. He was not only Kens attorney, but, he was also a good friend. He was always trying to look out for Kens best interest and at times could get a little over zealous. "What in the world is so urgent" Ken asked? "You won't believe this when I tell you" was his response. Ken was beginning to feel the worst was about to happen and braced himself for what he suspected was to come.

His friend explained that the company Ken had worked for at the time of his injury had been in touch. "Oh my God, now what" Ken inquired? They had wrote Ken off as soon as his doctor said he would never return to work and left him holding the bag, so to speak. They had shown no interest in helping or discussing a settlement in any way and even went so far as to say they were finished altogether with him. "Believe it or not, they are offering a settlement now" his friend told him. "You have got to be kidding, are you serious" Ken asked? "Completely" was the response from the other end of the line. "Is it a genuine offer or an insult" he asked? "I couldn't believe what they offered when they called" Dave told him. "Are you sitting down" he asked? "Yes" Ken told him, "should I be"? "You better be buddy, I don't want to hear you fall when I give you the details". His attorney told him what the company had offered and Kens heart almost stopped. "Are you kidding" he asked? "Not a bit" was his answer. The offer was far more than Ken could have ever imagined, as it were, he never imagined they would make an offer in the first place.

Discussing strategy and options took the best part of the next half hour. "What do we do" Ken asked his friend? "Should we take it or what"? Full of questions and no answers seemed to be something he had become accustomed to lately. "We have two options here" he told Ken. "We can either take this offer or roll the dice and hope for a better one, the call has to be yours though". This was tearing Ken in to, should he take the offer or see if they counter? It was a lot of money at stake here, and right now, money is what he and Nikki needed. And they needed it badly. "I don't know what to say or do Dave" he told his friend. "Help me here". His lawyer told him that the first offer is usually a "low ball offer" to see if you might let them off the hook easy. He seemed to think they were dealing with that in this situation. "It's entirely up to you but I would like to see if they make another offer" he told Ken. "It might be a roll of the dice, and, we both might be sorry we did this" he said, "but for some reason I don't think so". Deciding to take a chance, Ken told him to see if they would make a better offer and left it at that.

Knowing this could be a very big risk was first and foremost in his mind. The offer they made was more money than he ever thought he would have at one time. It would have went a very long way to make their dreams come true and could be a way for Nikki to either stop working completely, or at the very least, work part time is she so chose. This would haunt him until he was certain they offered more or came back with a take it or leave it response. He was praying it would be a better offer. He knew his nerves would be on the brink until he was sure of their future. This was a hard decision to make and he was now second guessing himself. Could he have been wrong in doing this? Maybe he should have just jumped at the chance to deposit a large sum of money in their bank and pay off all their debts. Again, a lot of questions and no answers.

The next two days were pure agony on Ken, he didn't even tell Nikki about the first offer. She would have jumped at the offer, of this he was sure. He just hoped this didn't undermine what they had found on their trip to Winterset. He hoped it didn't undermine them. Nikki could tell he was on edge and something was eating away at her husband. She just couldn't put her finger on what it could be. Ken had only told her that the lawyer said the company might be willing to offer a settlement. He couldn't bring himself to tell her that an offer had already been made and he had turned it down. She just wouldn't be able to understand how he could even consider doing something like that. He was beginning to wonder himself how he could do that. With all of this weighing heavily on him, Ken seemed to wander around in a distant daze lately. Not knowing how she could help, or what to say, Nikki sat by and just supported him as best she could. She too couldn't bear the thought of them losing what they had found in Madison County.

Several days passed and Ken was about to pick up the phone, and call his attorney to tell him he would take the offer when the phone rang. It was Dave. "Sit down Ken" he was told. "I have been negotiating for the last 3 days with these people, making every idle threat I could pull out of thin air, and, they made us another offer". "I have to tell you though, they were extremely clear that this would be a final offer". As his friend told him the figure they had offered, Ken dropped the phone. "Hello, hello, are you all right Ken" his friend called out? Gathering his wits and once again picking up the phone, he asked if this was for real. "It's for real my friend, very real". He agreed with the offer faster than the speed of sound. "I'll make all the arrangements" his friend said. "Congratulations Ken, you guys deserve this and you know it". The details were worked out and two days later Ken was receiving another call, this one from his bank. "Ken, we have a very, very large deposit here for you" the bank manager told him. They discussed how much to put in checking, how much in savings, and payed off a couple of small loans the bank held. Ken couldn't wait to tell Nikki, he had to do something that would be a total surprise.

He could only think of one that would be fitting. He quickly went to his computer and was soon searching public records. It took several hours but he found an address to the one person that could help, at least he hoped they could help, Francesca's daughter. He remembered Lucy telling them her name and for some unknown reason it stuck with him, unknown until now. He rapidly wrote a letter explaining that he would be interested in buying her Mothers old home and a few acres of ground. He disclosed to her how he came to know of the house and the story behind it. Sealing the envelope he rushed out to the porch as the mailman was coming up the drive. "I have one to go" he told the man. With his letter on it's way, he went back in and wrote Lucy again.

He told Lucy of his letter to Francesca's daughter and his sinister plan to get Nikki back to Winterset. About half way through the letter he decided this couldn't wait. He found the folded piece of paper the waitress had given him with the name Lucy on it and a phone number. His fingers almost trembled as he dialed the phone. A frail, raspy old voice answered and said hello. "Lucy, hi it's Ken" he told her. She recognized him right away and you could almost see her smile and hear the joy in her voice as they spoke. He told her of his plans and that he had wrote to Francesca's daughter hoping she would consider selling him the old house and a small parcel of ground. Lucy told him she had the girls number around somewhere and would call herself and propose the offer to her. He thanked her for her help and told her they might be seeing her again soon. That made the fragile old woman happier than she had been in a long time as she didn't have any friends since Francesca's death. With his plan at least put into action now, he started dinner and waited for Nikki to return from work. The evening was light and airy and Nikki could see a definite change in her husband. "OK, tell me what is going on here" she said as they sat down to dinner. "Why, whatever do you mean my love" he said? "You're up to something" she said and smiled, "I just don't know what...yet" she told him. He smiled and thought to himself, "I hope it stays that way too".

K. F. Coffman

Chapter 13

The next two weeks went by pretty much as usual and Ken gave Nikki no clues to what he might be planning. She had secretly asked their daughter and son and they told her they didn't know what she was talking about. "If he's up to something, he's keeping it very secret" her son told her. "He hasn't told me a thing" her daughter told her. Unknown to Nikki, Ken had received a phone call from Francesca's daughter, as he had enclosed his phone number with his letter. They discussed the possibility of him buying the old house and a small piece of land. She told him she would have no objections to the sale but would have to contact her brother and get his consent, as the farm was left to both of them when their mother died. He told her he understood and thanked her for her time. She assured Ken she would be back in touch with him soon as she and her brother were close and spoke almost daily. "I really don't think he will have a problem with the sale" she told him, "I just want him to be part of the decision". Understanding completely, and, assuring her that he would have it no other way they said their goodbyes. Hoping to have an answer soon Ken was again on pins and needles over the next couple of days. This time he was very careful to conceal his anxiety from Nikki. He didn't want her to ask questions or start playing detective.

The call came 3 days later and he practically jumped through the roof when he heard the woman's voice on the other end of the phone. She told Ken that she had spoke to her brother, had presented his offer, and, they were both in agreement to make the sale. She explained to Ken that they were actually quite happy to do so as neither of them had any plans on returning to the area. She was glad to see someone finally take an interest in the old place, and, asked if he was buying it to live in or tear down to build a new house. He hurriedly assured her that the old house would be fully refurbished, and, he planned on living in it. With price agreed upon, terms of the sale and amount of land he would purchase outlined, he told her Thank you and gave her his attorneys name and told her he would be in touch to finalize everything. "No, thank you" she told Ken, "I'm glad mom's old house is going to live again". They said their goodbyes and Ken extended an open invitation to stop by should they ever find themselves in the area again. "You know, I might just take you up on that" she told Ken.

Ken quickly hung up the phone and called his attorney. After telling David the whole story he couldn't wait to help his friend out. "I'll call her and make all the arrangements" he told Ken. "As soon as everything is ready to finalize, I'll call you for some signatures and a check" he said. Ken asked him to put a rush on this as he wanted to surprise Nikki but wanted to wait until he knew the deal was final. "I'll call right now" he told Ken and hung up the phone. Amazingly it only took Dave another week to completely put the deal together. Title search complete and papers ready to sign, Dave called Ken and told him to stop by with his pen and a check. "I'll be there in the morning" he told Dave. As soon as the papers were signed and filed and he knew the place was theirs, he would once again start making reservations in Winterset, Iowa. This time not to visit, as his wife would be led to believe, but to present her with her new home. The very place Robert and Francesca had led them to discover what they always knew was buried deep inside them. They just never imagined that what they would find would be so intense and beautiful.

After sending everyone off as uneventful as any other day, he sat down and called his bank. Making arrangements to have two checks drawn from his account, one for the children for the purchase of the home, and, one for his attorney for handling the legal matters, he finished dressing and was off. "Have you ever seen what color the top of your desk is" Ken asked his attorney as he entered his office? "What, you mean there's a desk under all of this" David replied with a smile. "I give up" Ken said as he found an empty chair. "Do you have everything ready for me" he asked as he sat down? "Sure, it's up here somewhere" his friend said teasingly. With fear starting to set in, Ken asked if he should come back next week. "Keep your shirt on pal" Dave replied with a grin and reached for a folder on top of the heap. "I have you right here" he said. They looked over the papers and he explained to Ken that the children had agreed to a much better deal than they had originally discussed for the same purchase price. They want to sell you the whole farm and be out from under it once and for all he was told. They went over all the details and clauses and Ken was assured that it was a simple sale that was totally in order. Ken signed by all the X's and handed David the two checks. "I'm sending the check to her overnight mail, is that all right with you" he asked Ken? "The sooner she gets it, the better" he said.

With the deal done and papers signed, they sat and enjoyed coffee and reviewed Kens plans for the old place. "Does Nikki have any clue what you are up to" Dave asked? "Not a clue, this is going to be a total surprise" Ken told him. "You better hope it's a good surprise" his friend told him. "If not, I'll be defending her for wringing your neck" Dave said as they both laughed. "She will love it" Ken assured him, "you won't have to worry about defending her for strangling me". "I'm sure glad of that" his friend said. They discussed family and how his youngest was doing in the service and relaxed and laughed for almost two hours before they were interrupted by the secretary. "You have court in an hour" she said as she pulled the door shut. "I'll file these since I'm going over to the courthouse anyway" Dave said. "Thank you for everything Dave" Ken said as he shook his friends hand and opened the door. "Anytime Ken, I'm always a phone call away" he responded as his friend closed the door. David somehow knew that his friends would be just fine now, as he picked up files and briefcase and headed for the door. He smiled to himself and thought that we all should be as fine as they would be.

Ken opened the front door and was met by his barking friend, tail wagging. Hi there little buddy he said as he picked up his small friend. Nikki hadn't returned from work yet, so, he knew she would have no idea that he had left the house. He had lost track of the time chatting and laughing with his friend, something that he hadn't done for a very long time. Ken just didn't get out much by himself since his injury and today felt especially good. He again had a huge surprise for his wife, one he was sure would make her extremely happy. He finished cleaning the kitchen and straightening up the house as she pulled into the drive. That was close he thought as he greeted her at the door. "Do I know you" he asked as she opened the door? "Are you sure you have the right house lady" he playfully continued. She laughed, hugged him and said that she hoped so. "If not my husband is sure going to miss me tonight" she teased in return. He asked if anything in particular sounded good for dinner and she told him whatever he made would be fine with her. Jr came home and asked what was for dinner and Ken told him they were going out for dinner tonight. "It's too hot to cook outside and it's too hot to cook inside" he told Nikki, "so, let's go out tonight". They were all in agreement and everyone quickly changed and prepared to leave.

Once in the car, they all made a unanimous decision on where to eat. Something that didn't happen very often Ken thought. The old fashioned drive-in they went to had classic and antique cars in the adjacent lot almost every night, tonight was no different. They ordered and ate then decided to stroll over and look at the old cars as Jr was restoring an old Chevy himself. "Maybe you can pick up a few ideas" Ken told him as they roamed from car to car. His son got so excited looking at the old vehicles as did Ken and Nikki. They would walk over to one and say "do you remember these" or "we used to have a car like this" it was always a nice outing when they came to see the cars, tonight was no exception.

During the drive home Nikki and Jr both squealed "ice cream". He knew that they would pester him until he agreed to stop, so, finding the next ice cream stand he pulled in. Nikki turned and looked at Jr, they both smiled from ear to ear like little children and said once again, "ice cream". He couldn't help but laugh as they made their way to the window. "May I help you" the clerk asked. "Yes, I need to feed these two little kids before I have a mutiny on my hands" he told her with a smile. With selections made and in their possession they headed once again for the car. "Oh no you two don't" he yelled. "I'm not turning you two lose in the car with ice cream, you set right there and eat it before we leave". As Nikki and her son exchanged licks of their treats Ken could only shake his head in total awe. It was like raising little ones all over agin with these two. They finished and left and once again headed home. "Are we there yet" the two teased as they pulled into the drive. "Yes we are here, now go in the house and get ready for bed" he told them. They laughed and joked and poked fun with each other as they all readied for bed. Goodnights said, and hugs and kisses exchanged, they went to their rooms and were soon deep in sleep. Just before drifting off Kenny looked at his sleeping wife and thought about just how lucky he truly was. He was soon fast asleep himself.

Chapter 14

The next morning after everyone was finally gone, he once again called his attorney. "Dave, could you do me a big favor" he asked his friend? "If it's legal" his friend shot back. Ken asked if he would check on the status of the paperwork he had filed and if he would please contact Francesca's daughter to confirm that she received the check. He wanted to make sure that everything was final and nothing could spoil his surprise before he sprung it on his unsuspecting wife. David assured him he would do all the follow-up work for him and make sure everything was in order. "Thanks Dave" he told him as they hung up. "I'll let you know either today or tomorrow at the very latest" he told Ken and hung up the phone.

It was later that same morning that Ken heard from his attorney. "Everything is done Ken, and I mean everything". "The place is yours, all yours". Thanking his friend he now knew it was time to start some serious planning. The first thing he needed to do was somehow get back to Winterset for a week by himself. How in the world could he do that without Nikki finding out? He did have some friends that lived about 2 hours northeast of them, but, he hadn't talked to them in months. He took a chance and called his friend and told him the most important parts of his dilemma. They were more than happy to help and agreed to cover for him should Nikki call looking for him. He thanked them and told them he would give them a number where they could reach him if anything came up. Now to make reservations in Winterset again.

Finding the motel receipt from the first trip was easier than he thought. He quickly called and reserved a room for a week, next was a rental car, and finally, he had to tell his wife he had to leave to help his friend. The story he and his friend decided on was one Nikki would easily believe. She knew his friend and his wife both were avid motorcyclists, and, would believe they had a minor accident that would leave them both with breaks and bruises. As soon as she returned from work he sat her down and explained that he had called their friends and found they had been in an accident. She of course was worried about their friends, but, Ken assured her they were fine. He continued with his story about having to go up to help them for a few days and she heartily agreed. As a matter of fact, she even offered to take some time off work and go with him. He quickly averted her plans by explaining how badly they needed the money and had lost a weeks pay when they went down to see Will. She knew he was right and decided that it would probably be better if she stayed and worked after all. He told her he would leave the next morning, as they had rented a car for him to make the trip with. "That was nice of them" she said as she helped her husband pack for his trip. "You make sure to take your medicine and cane". He promised to be the perfect patient and to be more careful than usual.

With Nikki and Jr off, the housework done and his bags packed and loaded he gathered last minute items and went to the car. Nikki had taken him to pick up the rental the night before so he wouldn't have to call a cab. The drive up was familiar and soothing and time passed quickly. Before he even realized it, his exit was two miles away. "That was quick" he thought as he exited the Interstate and headed south. Arriving in town, he went straight to the motel and checked in. After unloading his bags and freshening up a bit he knew where his next stop had to be, the diner. He had missed breakfast and lunch time was fast approaching, so, the decision was clear. As he walked through the door he was greeted with waves and hello's and went to their favorite booth. The waitress they had become so fond of was working today and waited on him with a smile that could light up the room. "Ok, what did you do with her" she asked as she approached the booth? He quickly told her what he was doing back and she couldn't be happier. He ate, paid the check and said goodbye and told her he would be back. He knew deep in his heart what his next stop had to be.

He drove along and remembered the roads well. It was as if it were only yesterday they traveled these roads in search of answers. He pulled into the drive and honked as he approached the house. He parked, walked to the door and before he could raise his hand to knock was greeted by a beaming smile. Lucy opened the door and gave the big man a hug and said "welcome back". They sat and talked and he told her about buying the house. She volunteered to help in any way she could. Thumbing through the phone book Lucy pointed out reputable contractors and people he could trust to do the work needed at a fair price. He called and made arrangements to meet several at the house the next morning. He promised to come back and told Lucy he would take her out to the house, if she would like. She told him she would like that very much and Ken told her it was a date then and headed once again for town.

The hardware store was the first stop, he desperately needed new locks for the doors. Even if they proved to be temporary. Picking up cleaning supplies and some brushes and rollers, he headed for the house. The afternoon sun was bright and the heat sweltering that day, but he was determined to do as much as he could before losing the light of day. The farmer he had met just weeks ago, was again in the field and pulled up to the fence as Ken approached. They talked and Ken told him about buying the farm. He asked Ken if he would farm the ground himself or would he be interested in leasing it to him as the last owners had? Ken assured him that nothing would change, except to whom he would pay the rent. They shook hands, and, Ken quickly drove up to the house. He went inside, and instantly felt that his decision to do this was indeed a good one.

He started to take old pieces of broken furniture out behind the house to a rubbish pile. Dusk was rapidly approaching and he knew he would soon lose all light. Securing the house the best he could, he headed back to town and stopped at the diner for a late dinner. After dinner he went straight to his room as he planned to arrive at the house very early the next day. He called Nikki and told her he had arrived and was fine and missed her terribly. They talked for some time and said goodbye, soon he found it hard to stay awake and slipped into bed.

Morning seemed to come early but was a welcome sight to Ken. He quickly showered, stopped at the diner for breakfast, then straight to the house. The first contractor was early and Ken respected a man that didn't leave the customer waiting. The man's name was Sam, a bit older than Ken, a short stocky man with greying hair and a huge smile. He would be the general contractor on the job and assured Ken that things would be done right, and on time. They shook hands and took a tour of the house, looking at the foundation and overall shape of the home. A plan of action was quickly agreed upon and Ken agreed on a price. Sam told Ken he would have a crew there first thing in the morning to get started. Cleaning, repairing broken windows and replacing doors to secure the house would be the first priority. Ken happily agreed and said he would meet him in the morning.

The electrician was the next to show up and he too toured the house and gave Ken a price to completely rewire and update the old home. They discussed such things as outdoor lighting, alarm systems and data ports for computer access. He would install ceiling fans and lights, complete with dimmer switches, and, bring the old home into the 21st century. Motion sensor lights would be installed in hallways and the stairway for added security and safety sake. They discussed service to outbuildings that would be built to replace some of the old ones there now. A garage would be added and service to it would be needed as well. The job wouldn't be as difficult as it may sound Ken was assured. The completed job would pass any inspection Ken would like to subject it to he was guaranteed. Coming to an agreement was quick and painless, the electrician too would start first thing in the morning.

Ken noticed a tractor, crawling at a snails pace, up the drive toward him. It was Jack smiling and waving his calloused hand. "Hi Jack" Ken said as the man stopped and stepped down from the seat. "I couldn't help but notice all the trucks coming and going, is everything ok"? Ken assured him everything was fine and told him of his plans to refurbish the old house. Jack made Ken an offer he couldn't refuse. He told Ken he was in the process of putting his mower deck on, and was going to clean up some of the grassy areas around the edge of the field, and, would be happy to mow the yard and tidy up the grounds. Ken quickly consented and thanked the man for the kind offer. The only payment Jack would accept was access to the cooler Ken had placed on the front porch. "Help yourself" Ken told the man. "There's iced tea, lemonade, and several kinds of soda in it Jack, take your pick". The big man smiled and told Ken that he would be back shortly as he reached in and retrieved an ice cold can of lemonade and opened it. "As soon as I'm done with the field, I'll do the yard and grounds around all the old outbuildings". "That way you can see what you are doing out there" Jack said. Ken thanked the man as he climbed up on his old tractor and started back down the drive.

It was going to start taking shape before he knew it he thought. Another truck was coming up the drive and Ken noticed it was the plumber he had called. Another tour followed and more prices agreed upon. All the workers would start the next morning and had estimated that it would take far less time to get the home back in shape than Ken had originally thought. He was very happy and anxious to see the place start taking shape again. The only contractors left to show up would be the roofer and heating and air conditioning people. They would be there later in the day and he found he had plenty of time to clean before they arrived. Something the old place was in dire need of, even with the broken windows and missing panes of glass, the floors needed to be swept and some dusting might reveal some fabulous old woodwork. That was one thing he had been adamant about during his meeting with the general contractor. The original wood floors and all the original woodwork would be painstakingly preserved and refurbished to original condition. There would be no compromising when it came to that he thought. This grand old home deserved that much he thought, and it would be done.

Armed with broom and dustpan, dust mask on his face and rubber gloves in place, he slowly approached the front door. Looking as if he were preparing for a battle, he opened the door and stepped inside. Looking to the left, then to the right, he decided the safest place to start would be the front hallway. After all, it was right in front of him. He busily swept and dusted and took as much of the debris and broken things lying about out to the pile he had started behind the house as he could carry or drag by himself. Knowing he would pay for it by morning with excruciating pain, he knew it would be worth the price he would have to pay. As he cleaned and dusted he noticed there were four fireplaces located on the main floor. Dusting the mantels revealed they were constructed of brown marble. "My God, these are gorgeous" Ken said aloud. Just a quick cleaning, was uncovering treasure after treasure in the sprawling old house. "Nikki will be astounded" he said to himself. The rumble of a vehicle woke him from his trance like state and he went to the front door to investigate.

A tall slender man with blonde streaked hair and hardened features was exiting a white van. The clanging and clattering Ken had heard was from the various ladders and things strapped to the roof of the vehicle. The man approached Ken, shook his hand and introduced himself. It was the heating contractor he had called. The man explained that he was early but hoped it would still be a good time to meet. Ken was more than pleased to show the man what he needed and what he expected for the old home. Armed with tape measure and pad of paper to make sketches of the layout of the ductwork, they entered the home. First stop was the basement, as they wandered around they noticed the foundation of the old home was in remarkable condition. "They don't make homes like this any more" the man told Ken. "I know and it's such a shame too" Ken responded. They finished the tour and had measurements to complete a rough sketch of what was to be done. The man gave Ken a price for the work and he agreed and asked how soon he could start. It was agreed that he too would begin in the morning. Laying out the ductwork and air vents would be first. Once they were done with that he told Ken, they could wait until some of the other workers were finished and come back and complete their work. They shook hands and the man drove back down the drive and disappeared. One down, one to go, Ken thought as he went back to his cleaning. The roofer would be the last contractor he had to meet today. He continued his cleaning awaiting his arrival. With broom swishing from side to side and the distinct sound of Jack and his mower in the yard Ken decided to clean as long as the daylight held out. Just then he once again heard a vehicle approaching and went to the front of the house to investigate. The roofer had finally arrived.

Ladders in place and windows opened on the second floor to grant access to the roof, Ken told the man that he hoped he didn't mind him watching from the ground as he looked things over. The man smiled and told Ken he didn't mind at all. He told Ken that he actually preferred it that way as he knew what he was looking for and where and how to step. He continued by telling Ken that he intended no offense and Ken assured him that none was taken. "You're the professional" he told the man as he watched from the ground. Gingerly stepping from spot to spot and pushing here and there with his foot, the man soon had covered the entire roof and was on his downward descent. The roof he was told was in far better shape and had weathered time much better than it looked. The repairs would be minimal and the cost not as gouging as Ken had guessed. A price was agreed upon and Ken was told they could start early the next morning. Ken also had the man price out all the flashing and guttering the old home would need and gave him that job as well. As they walked to the man's truck, they shook hands and he told Ken he would see him first thing in the morning. With all the contractors hired and plans to begin the next day he went back to his sweeping and dusting.

Day was fading fast and Ken knew he still had to stop at the bank in town and transfer money and open an account locally. Deciding that the mess would only get bigger as contractors performed their work, he went outside, found Jack and told him he was leaving. Jack said he would stop back, over the next few days, and if Ken needed anything he only needed to ask. Glad to have found another new friend in the area, he shook Jack's hand and told him he was leaving the cooler for him. "Feel free to help yourself Jack" he said as he walked toward the car. Jack shouted back that he would set the cooler inside before he left for the day and said he would see Ken soon. Ken waved and headed for town.

Ken arrived back in town to find the bank still open, he wasn't sure they would be as he wasn't yet that familiar with town. That too would change before he left for home he thought as he pulled into a parking spot and entered the bank. A tall, well built young man approached him, shook his hand and welcomed him to the bank. "You must be the man that all the buzz around town is about" the young man said. "What buzz is that" Ken asked? "You know small towns" the man continued, "everyone knows when something is going on". They sat at his desk and the man asked what he could help Ken with. "I need to open an account locally" Ken told him. They prepared all the necessary papers and called Kens bank, and had money wired into the new account. With this done, Ken thanked the young man and told him he hoped to see a lot of him. The man thanked Ken for choosing their bank and told him if he needed anything don't hesitate to ask. Ken knew from his grumbling stomach that it was past time to eat as he had overlooked lunch. He had eaten almost every meal at the diner and decided tonight he needed a change. He stopped and ordered a pizza and took his dinner back to his room.

Looking over the plans and estimates from the contractors was mind numbing and soon all the figures just ran together. Piling them on the table he picked up the phone and called Nikki. He was sure that she would be worried if he didn't call. "Hello" she answered as she picked up the phone. "Do you miss me terribly" was the only thing she heard from the other end of the line. She told him she did and they talked for almost a half hour. She said he sounded so drained and she was beginning to worry about him. He assured her that he was fine but was terribly tired as he didn't sleep well without her next to him. She told him she too knew the feeling as she tossed all night because of his absence. Not wanting to give anything away he told her he was going to bed but wanted to hear her voice before turning in for the night. "I love you baby" he told his wife. "I love you too, Ken" she said as she hung up the phone. Feeling better now that he heard her voice he got ready for bed. The only thing that kept eating at him was having to fool her like this. He just hoped this surprise would be one he wasn't going to regret.

Chapter 15

Morning again came much too quickly as he rolled and sat up in bed. Shaking off the night and heading for his medicine bottles on the counter, it was time for his first pill of the day. Something he never seemed to get used to, but, knew he needed to take them as the pain would cripple him without them. He showered and dressed and gathered his papers and plans before closing and locking the door. This morning he was going to eat at the diner, no fast food this morning. With a good breakfast behind him and a thermos of coffee in hand he again headed for their new homestead. He was the first to arrive and opened the house for the anticipated arrival of workers. Soon the drive was busy, and trucks and vans were scattered about everywhere. Workers scurrying about like tiny ants starting their varied tasks.

Ken had called and arranged to have the electricity and phone turned on this morning as well, and soon, workers were everywhere. At times it was almost comical watching them start and stop, and duck this board, or jump over that pile. With contractors coming from all corners of the house Ken felt as though he were being pulled in different directions at once. This was going to be a very long and tiring day he thought. A very long day indeed. He soon found himself in the thick of everything, and felt like a General, assigning his troops. Dumpsters were arriving and being sat in place and workers soon were busily filling them with pile after pile of rubbish. The tearing apart process was officially underway and he couldn't wait for the putting back together phase to begin. Ken practically beamed as he closed his eyes and could envision what the house would be transformed in to. Even if Nikki was a little less than ecstatic, he knew this surprise would be well worth it.

The day drug on and on, seeming to never end. Windows were picked out, that was one of the easy parts. He and Nikki had picked out windows for the home they live in now and Nikki always told him how much she loved them. With windows chosen and doors and shutter styles approved, the contractor was soon on his way to pick them up. Ken was told the windows and doors would be the first step, as that would secure the house properly once and for all. That made Ken feel more at ease and calmed his worries and fears a bit. The last thing he wanted was to start all this work, only to have some over zealous kids with more time on their hands than brains, destroy it. Without even noticing, another vehicle had pulled in during all the pandemonium. A well dressed, older gentleman approached Ken and asked if he was the new owner. He proudly told him he was and asked if he could help the man. "I hope I can help you" he calmly said. It soon was disclosed that he was a local insurance agent from town, something that had completely slipped Kens mind. He had thought of everything, contractors, bank, everything, and had completely overlooked the most important visit he should have made, insurance. They sat and discussed several plans and how Ken was going to use the farm. With all the information needed to give Ken a price, the man went to his car and pulled out a thick book. Upon his return he thumbed through pages and started jotting down notes and prices. Soon he had a price for Ken and it was far below what he might have imagined. Something he had found this area seemed to be popular for. He quickly signed the application and tried the phone. It was working, he thought he remembered someone coming to him and saying the phone was hooked up, but, during all this commotion he really couldn't swear to that either. He quickly called the bank and asked them to draw a check from his new account to pay for the insurance. The agent shook his hand and agreed that he would stop by the bank and pick it up and thanked Ken repeatedly. Now, Ken thought, I do have everything in place, I hope.

With only two days left in town before he again headed home, he hoped to make every minute count. The roofer assured him they would have their job complete the next day and would be out of the way. The plumber too was confident that he would have his portion of the restoration done by the end of the week. In time for Kenny to inspect everything before he left. The heating contractor would be done by tomorrow with the first phase of his work, and would too, be out of the way giving full access to the contractor and electricians. This was turning out better than he imagined and he felt he could now go back home and not worry so much about things.

The day continued and more decisions were made. Ken picked out lights that would be at the end of the drive near the road, lights that would line the drive on both sides and lights for the outside of the house. What outlets were needed where and how many and what was going to be ran for the outbuildings. With this complete, and, the questions of the removal and construction of a new barn and garage out of the way, he sat back and took a deep breath. The house was going to look great and the grandeur that the home had when first built, would be kept in as many ways as possible. The general contractor also knew that some items would have to be decided by his wife as he didn't want to leave her out of the process completely. He just wanted the house more in shape before he brought her back to surprise her. With evening soon sweeping over the horizon and turning a clear blue sky to shades of red and orange, everyone started picking up their tools and preparing to leave until the next morning. Ken too was about to leave for he had a stop to make before returning to town. He just had to stop and see Lucy and tell her of the progress he had experienced today. She would be happy to hear about it he was sure.

Ken pulled into the drive to find the friendly old woman he had become so close to, on the porch in her rocker. He smiled and waved enthusiastically as he exited the car and walked toward the porch. "Evening ma'am" he said as he went to the chair next to her. "How are you this evening Lucy" he asked as he took her small wrinkled hand in his. "I'm fine and how about you" she asked? He told her he was tired and felt completely drained from all the activity, but, he continued that he wouldn't trade the feeling for anything. She told him she knew exactly how he felt. He asked if she had ate and invited her to have dinner in town with him. She eagerly accepted as she doesn't get out much anymore. A trip to town would be nice indeed she thought. They gathered her handbag and a sweater just in case she got a chill, from the air conditioning, and headed off to dinner.

They talked and laughed and the tiny woman couldn't remember the last time she had enjoyed herself this much. After dinner Ken drove her home and asked if she might enjoy seeing the progress they were making on the old house, she said yes before he could finish asking. He smiled and helped her into the house and told her he would return in the morning and pick her up. She stood on her tiptoes and kissed his cheek gently as a tear formed in his eyes. "It's a date then" he said as he turned and walked to his car. With a wave and a hearty goodnight he was back on his way to his room. He slept soundly that night, even forgetting to call Nikki.

The next morning he showered, dressed and drove straight to Lucy's. She agreed that she would go with him, but, only if he allowed her to make him breakfast before they went. He eagerly agreed and told her he would help. After breakfast he helped the woman once again to his car and drove to the house. She had tears forming as they pulled up to the home. "I haven't been here since just before Franny passed on" she said in a broken voice. They had arrived before any of the workers, and for that he was thankful. It would give him time to show Lucy about, without having to dodge workers and materials. They went from room to room and she told him what she remembered about furnishings that were in each room and pointed out the rooms that Robert and Francesca favored. Entering the dining room, she took Kens hand and said "this is where they had dinner that last night they were together". She told him the story as Francesca had told her about the night she and Robert had sat in that very room and knew it would be their last time together. The story was sad, yet at the same time, somehow beautiful. One of a love these two people had shared, a love they had just found. One so pure and complete, and yet, they both knew it would be a love they would only hold in their hearts, never to be together again.

With workers starting to arrive Ken took Lucy home and told her he would return before he left the next day. She thanked him for taking her back to the house. She told him it was as if she had just visited Franny again and that felt very good. He waved and returned to the house to check on the workers. Another long and tedious day with roofers finishing their work, heating contractor finishing his work for now, and windows being fitted and installed. A lot had happened that day and the house was starting to look presentable once again. As the end of the day neared Kenny thanked and arranged payment for those finished with their work and discussed plans for the next day with those that weren't. With goodnights said and everyone gone, he made one last look around the house and decided to make an early evening of it himself. Besides, if he didn't call Nikki tonight he knew she would start forming a search party.

Settling once again for something fast for dinner, he again ate in his room and turned on the TV. He called Nikki and told her how sorry he was for not calling last night, but, told her he had been so tired he slept straight through the night. Not being pleased with him, for not calling, soon disappeared and gave way to a good feeling that he had gotten a full night sleep. Something she knew he didn't get very often, so, she quickly forgave him for not phoning her. She asked when he would be home and he assured her he would be there the next night. This seemed to make her very happy and he told her he was making an early night of it again tonight. They told each other they loved each other and said goodnight and soon hung up the phone. Tomorrow he would start back early, and he knew he had to stop and see Lucy before he left. He soon drifted off to another sound sleep.

He woke early the next day and stopped for a quick breakfast. Deciding to stop and see Lucy now instead of doing it later, he drove to her house. She was glad to see him, sad to hear he would be leaving tonight, but knew he would return and bring Nikki back next time. He told Lucy goodbye and drove to the house. By the time he reached the house, workers were already there and engrossed in their work. The windows would be in today and the new doors on, the roof was done and the guttering complete. The plumber was wrapping up his work for the time being, knowing there would be more work later when Nikki became involved. The ventilation system was complete for the time being and the electrician would be done by the middle of next week. It was coming together fast and the rewards would be enormous. He made his choices for the siding and trim. Steel siding in a light tan was chosen with hunter green trim. The house they live in now is the same color and they just adore it.

The insulation people were just finishing their work and placing those little plugs all over the outside of the house, to cover all the tiny holes they drilled to blow the insulation in. The poor house looked like it had a case of the chicken pox with all those dots. It was fast becoming early afternoon and Kenny knew it was time to head home. He made final arrangements with the general contractor to finish the work and had made arrangements for payment as well. With everything that he could do for the moment done, he shook hands and thanked everyone for all their effort and walked to the car. "I'll call you the middle of next week Ken and let you know how we are coming along" the contractor told him. Ken told him to remember to call during the day and waved and drove off.

The trip home seemed to pass rather quickly and before he realized it, he was pulling into his driveway. Nikki was already home and rushed out to help him carry his bags in. First he had to receive a big hug and kiss that she was keeping just for him. "What was that for" he asked as she grabbed him? "I missed you so much, that's what that was for" she told him. "Is that all right with you" she asked as she hugged him again? He assured her that it was fine with him and told her to never stop. They went in the house and put his things away. Later they returned the rental and stopped for dinner, just the two of them, as Jr had plans tonight. After dinner they went for a short drive and talked and just enjoyed being together after a five-day absence. They drove home and found they still had the house to themselves. They immediately took advantage of the situation and went straight to their room and shut and locked the door. That night he again made love to her so intensely and passionately that they became one soul.

Two weeks passed without anything out of the ordinary happening. Nikki felt like they were once again back to normal and it felt right. Ken received phone calls twice a week from his contractor with updates on the progress of the work being done. It was right on schedule he learned and no unforseen problems had been encountered. The windows and doors were in, the siding and trim were done. The house was now insulated and the electrician was done with his work for now. Sam told Ken that he would take pictures with his digital camera and e-mail them to him. Ken was delighted at the thought of getting a sneak preview of what the house had become. Ken told Sam Thank you, told him he would be back that next weekend and would call to have him meet them at the house. "This time I will have the boss with me" he told Sam. Sam told him he was looking forward to meeting her and they hung up.

Now it was finally time to let Nikki and the rest of the family in on some "well kept secrets". He called a local restaurant they only went to for special occasions and anniversaries and made reservations for that night. They agreed to have a private table big enough for their party and would arrange flowers that Ken would have delivered to the restaurant. "We will take care of everything and it will be perfect, we assure you" they told him. The next call was to his daughter, he told her to meet them at the restaurant at 6:00 this evening. She asked what was going on and he would only tell her that she would find out when they got there. With reservations made, flowers ordered and being delivered, he had only to wait for his wife and son to return home. He only wished his son Will could be here to enjoy this moment also.

Nikki pulled in the drive just minutes before their son. She had worked late today and would be glad to eat and relax, little did she know that tonight would be anything but ordinary. As soon as they both were in the house and asking what was for dinner, they noticed Ken was somewhat dressed up this evening. "Hey, what's up" his son asked? His wife could only nod in agreement with her son. "We are going out to dinner tonight and I need you two to clean up and change". "What's the occasion" they asked him? "You will find out when we get to the restaurant" was all he would tell them. "You look nice, where are we going" they asked? When he told them where they would be having dinner, they could only look at each other. "We only go there for something special" Nikki said. "So what is special about tonight" she asked? "I will answer all your questions later" he told them, "now go change and get ready" he said.

As they entered the restaurant and Ken told them he had reservations, a small voice cried out "hi grandma". Nikki turned to see her daughter, son- in-law, and grandchildren, all waiting for them to arrive. "Ok, now I'm starting to worry" she said, "please tell me what this is all about". They were shown to their table and seated and drinks were ordered. They looked over the menus and everyone ordered and waited for their meal.

White roses were set in little vases all about the table. Ken could tell that Nikki was completely taken back by all of this, as was the rest of the family. He decided they had been kept in the dark long enough. "Remember when I told you that the company might consider making us a settlement offer" he asked Nikki as he held her hand in his. "Yes I remember, did they make an offer" she asked? "They not only made an offer dear, but, we have the money already in the bank" he told his wife. With tears forming in her eyes, she asked if it would be enough to let them pay their bills? Ken told her it was more than enough.

Their meal arrived at the table and as they ate he told his family that he had paid off the house, the car, all the small loans they had, and every bill they owed. Nikki burst into tears and hugged her husband tightly. "I guess I just never believed they would do this" she cried. Jr and their daughter Lynn both hugged and kissed their parents and told them how happy they were for them. "It's about time you had something right happen for you" their son-in-law said as he too gave them hugs. Ken told Nikki that they had enough money now that she could quit work entirely, if she wanted to. They talked and enjoyed their meal and happy times had once again returned to this family. Fears and uncertainty of their future now fading as they finished dinner and left for home.

As they walked in the door Nikki turned to Ken and pulled him close and kissed him deeply. "Is it all true or am I dreaming and about to wake up" she asked him? "It's true my love, you're not dreaming" he told her as he playfully pinched her bottom. "Ouch" she said. "See, you're not dreaming" he replied. As they got ready for bed, Ken told her that he had a terrific idea. "How about us going back to Winterset for the weekend and telling Lucy the good news" he asked his wife? She was hoping he would ask, she too wanted very much to go back to the area. "Can you get a few days off work and we will go up for a whole week" he asked? "Jr, Lynn, and the family can drive up on Friday and spend the weekend with us" he suggested. "That way we still will have some time together, by ourselves, before they join us". She absolutely loved the idea and told him they could leave next Monday. She would tell her boss that she was leaving for a week. "If they don't like it, I guess they can get someone else to do my job" she said. "That's my girl" he told her as he settled her into his arms and kissed her goodnight. "I'll start making reservations tomorrow" he told her. "I love you Ken" she said as she kissed him goodnight. "I love you too, Nikki" he said as they drifted off to sleep.

Chapter16

Ken rose early the next morning as usual and started coffee, let the dog out, took his first pain pill of the day and waited for 5:30 to come. As he stood in the doorway watching his beautiful wife sleep, he found it very tempting to call her boss and tell him she wasn't feeling well today. Thank God this was Friday or he probably would have. Just then he noticed her stretching and rolling to see him standing in the doorway. She smiled and lit up the room, he couldn't help but think of how very lucky he was to have this captivating creature in his life. He truly was blessed he thought. "Do I really have to do this" she asked him as she stretched and yawned? "This time I can honestly say no honey, you don't have to if you don't want to".

Ken knew his wife too well though, she wouldn't leave her job like that, only making him respect her that much more. "You could give them two week notice today though" he told her. "I'll seriously think about that" she told him as she reached for her robe and headed for the shower. "Is coffee done" she asked as she headed for the bathroom? "Of course my love, isn't it always" he said as he went toward the kitchen. "There will be a cup on the table when you get out" he told her as he entered the kitchen. Shower, hair, makeup and teeth done she was now ready for that coffee. "If I quit my job, would we really be ok" she asked him in a very serious tone? Ken took a scrap of paper and wrote a number on it and slid it over to his wife. She took the paper and looked at what he had wrote on it. There was a number on it, and, it was a very, very large number, with a lot of zeros in it. Her eyes opened wide, her mouth dropped open and her hands shaking, she could only stutter. "What is this exactly" she asked? "That's our bank account balance right now" he said. She almost spit her coffee all over the table. "You mean, in our bank, right here, right now"? "Yes dear" he told her. "I gotta go to work" she said and picked up her things to go. "I'll call you during lunch" she said as she headed out the door.

He went about doing his daily tasks and watched the clock to make sure he didn't let his son oversleep. After getting his son off to work and joining his friends on the computer and letting them know he hadn't forgot them, he started to make plans for their return trip to Winterset. He called Lucy and told her that he and Nikki both would

81

be there Monday and would make her house the first stop. The old woman was ecstatic and asked Ken if she knew about the house yet? He told her no, that he was going to surprise her Monday when they drove out to see it. "I just know she will love it" she told him. "I wish I could see her face when you tell her" Lucy said. "You will" he told her, "you are going with us". This made her very happy and now more anxious than ever for their return. Ken told her they would see her Monday and hung up the phone.

Before he realized how late it had become, the phone rang. It was Nikki and she asked if he had made the reservations for the motel yet? "No, I haven't babe, I was just about to" he told her. "Make them for tonight" she told him. "I want to go as soon as I get home, I don't want to wait". He could tell that something was wrong and asked if she was ok. "I told my boss that I was going to give a two-week notice and that I wouldn't be here at all next week" she told him. "And he said what" Ken asked? "He told me to just leave today and not worry about coming back". "I'm sorry honey, I didn't mean for this to happen" he told his wife. "I couldn't be happier" she told him. "I might not even last the whole day, who knows". She seemed bubbly and happy and he could hear a sound of relief in her voice. If this makes her happy he thought, he was going to be happy with her. "It's up to you love, if you want to come home now, then just do it". "You know I am behind you all the way in whatever you decide" he told her. "Start packing, and I mean now" she said. "I'm coming home" she said as she hung up the phone.

Ken hurriedly packed enough clothes for a week for them both. If they needed any more than that, they would just have to do laundry while they were there. He packed makeup, toiletries, his medicine, and everything he could possibly think that they might need for a week stay. He was still on the phone with the motel as she walked in the door. She looked like a wrongly convicted person that had just been released. She had a look of sheer joy and absolution to her that he couldn't remember seeing in a very long time. "Are we ready to go" she yelled as she walked in the room? He informed her that he was still on the phone with the motel and would be done soon. It was only 1:00 in the afternoon and it would only take them 2 hours for the trip. They had plenty of time and he told her to shower and change and they would be off. She eagerly complied as she started taking off her clothes and tossing them about on her way to the bathroom. He finished his call and started picking up her clothes behind her as he went to their room and laid out fresh clothes for her.

As she showered, he looked for his keys to the house, he had brought them back with him from his last trip. Finding them and sticking them in his pocket, he went back to the kitchen to pack a small cooler with sodas for the trip. As Nikki dressed and did her makeup and hair for the second time today, he loaded their bags into the car. He loaded his wheelchair this time, as this wouldn't be just a 2 or 3 day trip and he might need it. With the car loaded and everything ready for departure, he quickly called their daughter and told her they were leaving now. "I'll explain later when I call to give you the number we will be at" he told his dumbfounded daughter. "Ok, be careful" was all she could manage and he hung up the phone. "Are we ready to go now" she hollered as she quickly headed for the door? "Yes my dear, we are finally ready" he told her as he locked the door. "We have to stop at Jr's job and let him know we are leaving now" he told her as they climbed into the car. "I know, I just want to go and I want to go now" she told him as she scooted close to him and snuggled up to his side.

Ken walked in and found his son working the front counter of the store he worked in. "We are going back to Winterset now" he told his son. "Your mom just can't wait, and wants to go now". "Does she always get her way" Jr asked? "Never mind" he told his dad, "I already know the answer to that" he said with a smile. Ken reached in his pocket and handed his son a bundle of money and told him that if he wanted to come up this weekend, he would call tonight and give him directions. "That would be great, I would like that" Jr told him. "What time will you call tonight"? Ken told him they would call around 9:00 tonight and to make sure he was home. He assured his dad that he would be there and told him to have a safe trip. Ken waved as he walked out the door and went to the car. "Are you sure you are ready for this" he asked as he took her hand in his? "I'm more than ready" she told him as she again snuggled next to her husband, and they were off.

The trip was becoming so familiar to Ken that he was almost certain he could make it in his sleep by now. As they exited the Interstate and headed south toward Winterset, Nikki was becoming even more anxious. She was like a small child waiting to pounce on presents Christmas morning. They were soon pulling into the motel and he quickly went in and registered and got their key. They parked and started taking bags to the room. With the car unloaded and the bags unpacked and put away in their room, it was rapidly approaching dinner time. Nikki looked at her watch and started bouncing up and down. "Are you all right" Ken asked as he looked at her with a puzzled look? "Diner" was all she chanted, over and over. He just laughed and said "yes baby, we are going to the diner for dinner". She jumped and cheered and hugged her husband, almost knocking him to the floor. It did him good to see his bride this happy, and, he hoped it was only the beginning. He kissed her and hugged her tight and asked if she was ready to go. She almost knocked him down on her way out the door. "I'll take that as a yes" he said as he closed and locked the door.

As they entered the diner everyone waved and said hello, something she had missed since they left. "I love this place" she said as they slid into "their booth". "Their" waitress came to the table with glasses of water in hand, as she sat them down, Nikki jumped up and hugged her. "I knew you would be back" she told them as she hugged Nikki. "I sure have missed you two" she said. Nikki excused herself for the bathroom and said they would order when she came back. The woman asked Ken if he had told her about the house yet? "Not yet" he told her, but told the lady she would find out tonight. "I'll spread the word so no one slips and tells her anything then" she said as she walked away. "Thank you" he whispered as she walked from table to table to refill coffee cups and chat with the patrons. Nikki was practically skipping as she came back to the booth. He could only smile, it gave him a feeling of completeness to see Nikki this happy. It had been such a long time since she had felt like this, and he of all people, knew she deserved it. They quickly ordered and waited for their dinner to arrive. After they were done Nikki decided, she just had to have dessert, and he wasn't about to deprive her of that. Finally done, tip left and check paid they waved goodbye and started for the door. The friendly old waitress just smiled and winked and several of the regulars that Ken had befriended on his last trip gave him the thumbs up sign.

The drive to Lucy's seemed quicker than usual, maybe because Ken had become so familiar with the roads. As they entered the driveway, they could see Lucy standing on the porch waving frantically. Nikki jumped from the car before it came to a complete stop and ran to the porch. She hugged Lucy and both women had tears in their eyes by the time Ken joined them. "I missed the two of you so much" Lucy told them. "We weren't going to come until Monday, but, I just couldn't wait" Nikki told her. She told Nikki to come inside and help her with tea and they would sit and talk a while. They quickly emerged with a tray of fresh tea and sat on the porch for a while. Deciding that now was as good a time as any to spring his gigantic surprise on Nikki, before it got any later, or darker. Ken asked Lucy if she would like to go for a drive by Francesca's old house. She smiled and eagerly said she would love to. Nikki helped her into the car and they headed toward the house.

As they neared the house, Nikki could see that there appeared to be lights on at the home. "Look" she said, "there are lights by the road and lining the drive". "Don't tell me someone finally bought the place" Nikki said with a definite sadness in her voice. As he glanced over the seat, he could see that Lucy was practically giddy with excitement. She could barely contain herself. "Lets drive up and check it out" Ken said as they entered the drive. "Did you hear anything about the house being bought Lucy" Ken asked as they neared the house? "Well goodness no" she said as they came to a stop in front of the house. "It's beautiful, absolutely beautiful" Nikki said as she wandered around as if in a trance.

With Lucy on her arm they slowly walked around the house. Ken came up to them as they stood in front of the porch, and just looked in awe. "Well, what do you think" he asked Nikki as he put his arm around her waist? "Like I said, it's beautiful" was all she could manage to say. Lucy finally lost control and could hold back no longer. She laughed and laughed and just couldn't stop. Ken too lost it and started to laugh uncontrollably. "Ok you two, what is going on here, someone spill it" she demanded. Ken couldn't wait any longer, he reached in his pocket, took out a set of keys and handed them to her. With tears in his eyes, he lowered himself to one knee. "I tried to think of a way to give you back even a small portion of the happiness you have given me all these years". "The only thing I could think of, was to give you the most beautiful thing I could find, my love, my respect, my undying devotion, and my heart just didn't seem to be enough Nikki, so, I wanted to give you something more". As tears streamed down her face, and Lucy's, he continued. "The only thing I could think of, that would even come close my love, is this house".

"So it is with my heart and soul that I give this house to you". He stood, took her in his arms and kissed her with such passion that it shook her to her very being.

With everyone now in tears, Ken led them to the front door and told Nikki to open it. She inserted the key and turned the lock, as the front door swung open she caught her breath. The interior had been scrubbed and cleaned and everything that could be finished was. The floors, the woodwork, the fireplaces all looked new. Once inside Nikki went from room to room and turned on lights and marveled in the transformation the home had gone through. She couldn't believe it was the same house they had wandered through only a short time ago. One that was in such disarray and in need of so much. Now as she stood there, taking in all of this, she could only think of one thing. It was hers. She turned to her husband, walked slowly over to him and hugged him tightly. "This is the most caring, loving thing you have ever done for me Ken, Thank you my love".

They showed the rest of the house to Lucy and Ken pointed out things that still needed to be done. "I didn't want to finish it completely sweetheart, I wanted you involved in the completion of it" he told her. Lucy found it utterly amazing, she never thought she would live long enough to see the house in liveable condition again. It was a miracle she thought. They turned on the outside lights and walked the grounds. The new barn and garage were up and the wiring and lighting were complete. Lucy appeared to be getting a bit weary so they decided to take her home.

As they drove toward her house she asked if they would live here or rent the home to someone else? Nikki turned in her seat and took Lucy's tiny hand in hers, and told her that she was going to get new neighbors. The old woman absolutely lit up the car with her smile. "I would love that" she said as they pulled in her drive. As Nikki helped her into the house and made sure she was safe and sound, she told her they would see her again in a few days as she was anxious to get started on her new home. She said she understood and kissed Nikki's cheek as she closed the door. As they drove back to their room Nikki asked how he had arranged all this without her knowing anything? "It wasn't easy" he assured her as he breathed a sigh of relief. Soon they were back in the room and began to get ready for bed. "So what's next" she asked Ken? "Well, tomorrow we call the contractor, have him meet us at the house, and you make the final decisions on the home" he told her. "I can hardly wait" she said as they cuddled and fell off to sleep.

K. F. Coffman

<u>Chapter 17</u>

They rose early that next morning and quickly showered and dressed. Ken made a call to Sam and asked if he would meet them at the house? Sam agreed and said he would see them in about two hours as he wanted to stop for breakfast first. Ken told him they too were going to the diner for breakfast, if he would like to join them. He gladly accepted and told Ken, he would meet them there shortly. They drove to the diner and found their favorite booth available. Nikki slid in next to Ken as they knew they would be joined for breakfast this time. Their favorite waitress soon appeared with fresh coffee, something they needed badly this morning. Nikki got up on her knees, leaned over and told her about the house. "You finally told her" she asked? Nikki slapped his shoulder and said "what does she mean you told me finally"? He could only sink in the booth as the entire diner clapped and cheered. Ken stood and took a bow as Sam came through the door. "Did I miss anything" Sam asked? Ken shook his hand and introduced him to his wife. "Sam, I would like you to meet the boss, my wife Nikki". Sam shook Nikki's hand and told her, it was nice to finally meet her. "Now we can get some work done at that old house" he told Ken. "Now that the boss is finally here". "Oh thanks Sam" Ken said as they ordered breakfast.

They ate and paid the check and Sam followed them to the house. They walked through the rooms and Sam pointed out to Nikki what needed to be done yet. "I have been waiting to meet you to get the final say so on this job" he told her. They sat and picked out carpet colors, decided on ceramic tiles in the kitchen and what color they would be. Nikki picked out cabinet styles and chose to have them white with glass doors. She showed Sam where she wanted the island and how big it was to be. She went over all the unfinished details that had to wait until she became involved in the project. Within two hours they had made all the final decisions and Sam told her he would be there first thing Monday morning to start. As Sam was leaving two other trucks pulled up in front of the house, it was the plumber and heating contractors.

Ken and Nikki followed the man up to the bathroom and Nikki once again chose fixtures and colors. Deciding on corner whirlpool tub and corner shower stall, Nikki chose vanity size, color, and where it would be placed. After half an hour the bathroom was now completely planned out, and the plumber would too, be back Monday morning to start. As Nikki worked with the plumber, Ken and the heating contractor went to the basement and Ken picked out brand and type of equipment to install and what extras they would require. Monday would prove to be a very busy day as everyone would be back to finish the work they had begun weeks earlier.

Another car pulled in the drive and came toward the house. It was Jr, Ken had called him the night before and gave him directions to the home.

Jr pulled up, got out and looked around as if he were lost. "What's wrong" Nikki asked her son as she met him by his car? They told the boy the whole story as they showed him the house. Jr was fascinated with the home and asked his parents what they planned on doing with the house they have now? Ken told his son he had plans for the house, but, promised him he wasn't going to sell it. With afternoon soon fading, they went back to town to get a room for their son. With him in the room next to them they took him to their favorite restaurant in town, the diner.

They entered the diner, waved at friends and went straight to their booth. Their waitress was off tonight so they ordered quickly and ate. After dinner they drove their son to two of the nearby bridges as it wasn't yet dark. He loved the bridges and could see why his parents had fallen in love with this area. Back at the motel Ken and Nikki sat with their son and discussed the possibility of him renting the house they had now from them. He told his parents that he and two of his friends had been looking for a house to rent and would be happy to rent theirs. Ken and Nikki both knew his friends and trusted them completely. They talked about it more and said the details could be worked out later. He was so glad that his parents trusted him, and his friends, enough to let them take over the house. He thanked them for understanding and hugged them and told them goodnight, as he headed toward his room. Goodnight son, they both said and prepared for bed themselves.

The next two days were spent showing their son the bridges and other attractions of the county. He loved the area almost as much as his parents and could understand how they would want to stay. As he prepared to leave for home he told them not to worry about anything, he would take good care of everything until they got home next week.

He agreed to come back next weekend and he would bring his friends back with him this time. He thought they would love the area and the new house as much as he did. "I love you Mom and Dad" he said as he drove away. They waved as they watched their son drive out of sight. The next day would be a hectic one as all the workers would meet them at the house to begin the finishing touches the house still needed. They ate dinner, went for a short drive and made an early evening of it. They went back to the room early and watched TV before nodding off to sleep.

They met the workers at the house early the next day, and, over the next two days found themselves more lost and confused than ever. The work was coming along faster than they had hoped and new appliances were being delivered and hooked up. They decided to take the next day off and go shopping for new furniture for the home. They left early the next morning and drove into Des Moines. They found everything they wanted and were having all the new things delivered Friday. They have been assured that all the work would be done by then. As they drove back, they decided to leave for home in the morning and pack. They would have to do it sooner or later and this seemed like the proper time. As they pulled back in the drive to the house, they agreed to designate rooms and plan where things would go. They walked from room to room, and, for the most part, left things as they were. Of course the kitchen and dining rooms would be left untouched, as would the 3 bedrooms upstairs. Francesca's old office would now be Kens new computer room and office. He found himself more in need of a home office, as he had been dabbling in some investments since their windfall. He was doing rather well at it, something he could never see himself doing before his injury. The parlor would remain a formal style living room, and, the room they found the broken old TV in, would now become the family room. The wall in the pantry was taken out to make way for a main floor laundry and mud room. The room they guessed was Francesca's old sewing room would now become a fourth bedroom. The mystery room they found by the bathroom, would now be used as a dressing area.

The entire third floor now housed two more bedrooms and another bathroom. They wanted plenty of bedrooms just in case kids and grandchildren came in for weekend visits. They both decided they didn't want company sleeping on floors and couches. They knew they would have no time to waste on their return trip home, as new things were being delivered Friday and they wanted to be there for that. They drove home early the next day and rented a truck before going to the house. They spent most of the day packing what they wanted to take. Mostly pictures, clothes, memorabilia that they had collected over the years and personal items. They were leaving the furniture, for the most part, for their son Jr to use. The dishes and bedding and anything else they could think of that he might need was left also. With the truck packed and animals in the car, they once again headed for Winterset. This would be their last trip from here to there, they sadly thought. This trip would signal an ending yet a fresh beginning at the very same time. They made this trip with a sort of sadness and closure, yet, a newfound hope and happiness. It was made with mixed emotions, that much was clear. They stopped and told their son they were leaving again for Winterset, and that they had gotten their things from the house. He too, had a sort of sadness about seeing his parents go, but, knew it was the best thing for them. They told him about leaving him the furniture and things, and told him anything they left behind was his now. A tear formed in their sons eye, as he hugged his parents and saw them drive away.

They arrived back at the new house just as dusk was settling over the land and quickly unpacked and dropped off the rental truck. They were tired, weary, and definitely hungry. They went once again to the diner for dinner. Something they had become very accustomed to lately, and, were sure it would be a favorite spot for them for years to come. They ordered their meal and sat in total silence for a while. As their meal came, they noticed their favorite waitress was approaching them. It must have been her night off as she didn't have her apron on or order pad in hand. They sat and talked and enjoyed a cup of coffee. She could see that something seemed to be wrong and asked if she could help. They told her about moving their things from home up to their new home and she fully understood. "It sure can be a sad thing to move like this" she said. They talked a while longer, and, the couple decided to make a some what, early night of it. Tomorrow would prove to be hectic and trying, of that they were sure. They paid their check and with goodbyes said, they headed for their room. As they sat in the room, Ken kneeled down before his wife and took her hands in his, and looked deep into those beautiful eyes of hers. "You know" he said, "tonight will be a lot of lasts". "What do you mean" she asked? "Well, tonight will be the last night in the motel, the last night of daily meals at the diner, the last time we will call our old house home, and the last time we will travel here as visitors". "Tomorrow" he continued as he became lost in those eyes of hers, "tomorrow will be a lot of firsts". "It will be the first day in our new home, our first meals there also, the first time we will be considered residents of Madison County, and the first time we will have the kids over for the weekend". "Sounds like a lot of firsts and lasts" she told him as tears filled those beautiful eyes, he loved so much. He pulled her close and kissed her deeply and passionately. "I just hope that I've made you happy" he said to her as he trembled. "You have made me happier than words could say Ken, don't ever forget that or doubt that" she told him as she held him tight. They soon drifted off to sleep, thinking about what tomorrow would bring.

K. F. Coffman

Chapter 18

They rose before dawn the next morning and quickly showered and packed, knowing they had to meet people at the house first thing this morning. They checked out and told the lady at the desk that they wouldn't need the room tonight after all. She told them she knew they were moving into the old farm but didn't know if it was ready or not yet. Nikki beamed as she told the woman that she was moving in today. She was so proud of her husband for what he had done for her, even if he did have to conceal it from her like he did. As they drove to the house they agreed they just had to stop later and see Lucy, and tell her the good news about the house being done and them moving in. Nikki volunteered to go pick their friend up as soon as the furniture was delivered and the unpacking was done. "I want her to see it when we are done, see it as it will be in all it's splendor" she said. He couldn't think of a more fitting way to show Lucy the finished product of all their efforts. As they unlocked and opened the front door they were soon greeted by the mess they had left from the night before. "I guess I didn't realize we left things in such a mess last night" Nikki said as she looked about. "Me either honey, I guess I thought we were neater than this". They quickly set about unpacking boxes and putting things away, waiting for the workers to return for last minute details and the furniture to arrive.

As they emptied boxes, Ken ran them out and threw them in the dumpster, so they could be hauled away today. Soon they were officially unpacked and moved in, for the moment anyway. The workers were beginning to arrive and finish last minute details and cleaning. Before they realized the time, a truck was pulling up with all their new belongings, asking where she wanted this and where that would go. The rooms quickly filled with furniture and Ken and Nikki arranged things as they were brought in and set in place. Time seemed to fly that day and before they knew it, workers were done and gone, furniture was in place, beds made, and dishes in her china cabinets to be proudly displayed. Taking a break, they called their son and daughter to see if they still planned on coming out for the weekend. Jr was coming and bringing his two new roommates with him, Lynn and her family said they wouldn't miss it for the world. They would all arrive by 7:00 that evening, Lynn was given details as Jr knew how to find the house already. Nikki's next phone call was to Lucy, and she was more than eager to have the first, finished tour of the house. Nikki told her she would be there in just minutes and quickly gathered her keys. As Nikki drove off to fetch Lucy, Ken walked through the house and marveled in its new splendor. His mind wandered back to the days that Francesca lived and loved in this old home, wondering if she would be pleased with what he had done to it. He wondered if she would be happy that he rescued the old home from a fate that was inevitable. He could only imagine, but was somewhat sure that Robert and Francesca both would be pleased.

He was awakened from his daze by the sound of a car pulling into the drive, looking out the front he could see it was Nikki returning with Lucy. He quickly met the car and opened the door for Lucy, as he helped her out he received a huge hug, a kiss on the cheek, and a heart felt "I've missed you both". As they toured the home, Lucy was utterly amazed at the end result. "Franny would be pleased" she said as they sat at the kitchen table. "I was hoping you would say that" Ken told her. "I was just thinking about that as I looked about before you arrived" he told her. "Franny would be proud of you both" she assured them. As they sat, talked and enjoyed fresh glasses of cold ice tea they heard a car approaching. Nikki went to the front and announced that the kids were there. As the cars were parked and people started filling the home, they were quickly introduced to Lucy. They talked and laughed well into the night before Ken drove Lucy home. "That was one of the best nights I can remember in a very long time" she told him as he helped her into the house. "It surely won't be the last either Lucy" he told her as he made sure she was safe and sound before leaving. The rest of the weekend was the best Ken and Nikki could remember in years. It was memorable and full of love and togetherness, something they lacked before coming here. As their son and his friends prepared to leave, and, hugs and kisses were distributed, he told his parents to expect to see a lot of him. "We wouldn't have it any other way Jr" his dad told him.

With the kids and grandchildren gone, the weekend over, and Lucy called to make sure everything was fine, they settled in for their first real night together in the house. That night they made love so intense and filled with passion that they were glad they weren't at the motel. They were both sure they would have woke the whole place. Ken kept his promise to Lucy too, she was a frequent visitor until she too passed on to join her friend Francesca. Their son Will came to visit them as soon as he was permanently stationed and even asked his parents if he could get married there. Of course they agreed. All their children and grandchildren visited often and friends stopped by all the time. The old house was once again alive and filled with love, as were it's occupants. Ken and Nikki seemed to grow stronger and closer with each passing day, and, the spirit of Robert and Francesca seemed to be right at home with them. They visit the Roseman and Holliwell bridges faithfully and take fresh flowers to the secret hideaway that Lucy had revealed to them, on a regular basis. Days find Ken at work in his office on his computer and Nikki is always planting and tending to something in her flower gardens. The old house and grounds have never looked better. Nights would find the two of them always together, no matter what they were doing. And every night before going to bed they would dim the dinning room lights, find a jazz station on the radio, and give the lovers that led them here, led them to each other, the privacy they so needed. It has been said that late at night, if you watch real close, you can make out the distinct shape of a couple dancing in that dining room. And this Ken and Nikki believe, they just don't bother their honered guests.

K. F. Coffman

About The Author

The author is a 48 year old husband, father of 3, and Grandfather of 3 that finds himself disabled due to a back injury. Unable to work, and nothing but time on his hands, he decided to take an English Comp teachers advice, write. This is his first attempt to write anything other than business proposals and book reports, and, it seems he has found his true calling. He confesses that it took him a whole 10 to 15 hours to complete this book, and if that isn't amazing enough, it is his first and only draft. If his first attempt is this good, who knows what is in store for him, or us, next.

Printed in the United States
1209900001B/321